"It Seems That No One At Your Agency Ever Takes Us Seriously, Mr. Becker."

Eli was uncomfortably aware that he had failed to behave with appropriately professional conduct. He had openly refused to believe the client's claims. Not only that, but he was becoming *in*appropriately interested in the client—who was currently looking at him as if he were a suspect piece of meat. He sighed and resolved to remedy all of those errors—especially the last one.

"Look, Fiona..." he said hesitantly, and he put his hand on her shoulder.

She looked directly up into his face, and he forgot his words. His gaze shifted to her mouth, pink, full, soft, inviting, enticing....

Before he knew it, he was leaning forward to kiss her, wanting to taste her sweet and spicy lips.

She jumped away from him just before they kissed. His eyes flashed up to meet hers, and he saw surprise there for an instant before it was replaced by total outrage.

"Get out of my house this instant!"

Dear Reader:

Happy Holidays from all of us at Silhouette Desire! This is our favorite time of year, so we've pulled together a wonderful month of love stories that are our gifts to you, our readers.

We start out with *Man of the Month* Luke Branson in Joan Hohl's *Handsome Devil*, which is also a sequel to *The Gentleman Insists*, February 1989's *Man of the Month*.

Also, look for three wonderful stories filled with the spirit of the season: *Upon A Midnight Clear* by Laura Leone, *The Pendragon Virus* by Cait London and *Glory, Glory* by Linda Lael Miller. Rounding out December are the delightful *Looking For Trouble* by Nancy Martin and the tantalizing *The Bridal Price* by Barbara Boswell. All together, these six books might make great presents for yourself—or perhaps for a loved one!

So enjoy December's Silhouette Desire books. And as for 1991 . . . well, we have some wonderful plans in store—including another year of exciting *Man of the Month* stories! But more on all that in the new year. In the meantime, I wish each and every one of you the warmest seasons greetings.

All the best,

Lucia Macro
Senior Editor

LAURA LEONE

UPON A MIDNIGHT CLEAR

SILHOUETTE *Desire*®

Published by Silhouette Books New York

America's Publisher of Contemporary Romance

SILHOUETTE BOOKS
300 East 42nd St., New York, N.Y. 10017

Copyright © 1990 by Laura Resnick

ISBN: 0-373-05610-9

First Silhouette Books printing December 1990

Books by Laura Leone

Silhouette Desire

One Sultry Summer #478
A Wilder Name #507
Ulterior Motives #531
Guilty Secrets #560
Upon a Midnight Clear #610

Silhouette Special Edition

A Woman's Work #608

LAURA LEONE

has been an unemployed actress, an unqualified language teacher, and an undisciplined student. She has lived and worked in five countries and hopes to quadruple that number before she retires. Named the "Best New Series Author of 1989" by *Romantic Times*, Laura likes writing for a living because she can sleep late, avoid rush-hour traffic, and work in her slippers.

This one is for my parents,
the Big Guy and the Boss Lady,
who raised me at a kennel where
I have spent many a Christmas season

One

Fiona Larkin twisted the strap of her purse tensely and wondered again if she was doing the right thing.

Arthur Morgan, the elderly president of Morgan Security Inc., regarded her seriously for a moment and then said, "I'm going to have Elijah Becker join us. He's one of my best men, and I think he should be included in this discussion. Will you excuse me for a moment?"

Fiona nodded and watched Morgan leave the office. She had noticed his heavy limp earlier, but she wasn't going to be rude enough to ask him about it.

Then nervous energy propelled her out of her chair. She started pacing around Arthur Morgan's impressive office, reviewing recent events, organizing her thoughts. Above all else, she didn't want to sound silly or hysterical when she explained her reasons for being here.

She had certainly come to the right place, she reflected. In addition to the Morgan agency's special relationship with Fiona's employer, one wall of Morgan's office was covered with plaques and citations giving ample proof of the agency's excellence. Her eyes followed the indications of the man's successful military career, various appointments in the defense department, licensing to operate his own private company of investigators and security consultants and awards of merit for the agency.

In fact, now that she thought about it, Morgan and his men might well consider her problem too piddling to deal with. Maybe she *shouldn't* have come here.

Fiona turned impatiently away from the intimidating accumulation of qualifications. She went to stand by the window where she gazed unseeingly out at the Virginian suburb of Washington, D.C.

Of *course* she should have come. She remembered her terror last night. She remembered the frustration that came later when the police explained there was little or nothing they could do to help her. What's more, Arthur Morgan had greeted her courteously and hospitably.

She glanced up as Morgan reentered the office.

"He's just finishing a phone call," Morgan explained, "and then he'll be right in. Can I get you some coffee?"

"No, thank you." She'd probably go through the roof if she added caffeine to her overcharged system.

Morgan limped to his chair and sat down again. He smiled at her in a fatherly way. She took a seat, too, wishing this other man would finish his phone call so they could get on with it.

"Have you got much Christmas shopping left to do?" Morgan asked kindly, trying to put her at ease.

"No," she said truthfully.

"Got it all done?"

"Yes." She had only needed to buy one gift for the upcoming staff Christmas party.

"Did you have a lot to do?" Morgan persisted.

"Not really." Although she didn't like the topic, she asked politely, "Do you have much more to do?"

He shook his head. "Luckily my wife does most of it."

"Oh."

Relief poured through her when the door opened. Now she could get down to business instead of talking about how many Christmas presents she didn't need to buy. She turned toward the newcomer.

He was gorgeous. Not just handsome or attractive or prepossessing, but absolutely stunning in a totally masculine and unconscious way. He was smiling and saying something to the secretary as he stood with the door open and one foot in the office.

"Merry Christmas, Eli," the woman said with abundant warmth.

"Have a good one. I know *I* will," he answered. He nodded to her and closed the door. As soon as he saw Fiona, he stopped and stared for the briefest of moments, as if he were surprised to see her there. Then he glanced at his superior. "Sorry, Arthur, I didn't realize you had a client waiting with you."

"That's all right. Let me introduce you. This is Fiona Larkin, the assistant manager of Oak Hill Pet Motel."

It took a moment for recognition to register on the man's face. "The boarding kennel?"

"That's right. Fiona, this is Elijah Becker."

Fiona gave Elijah Becker a brief handshake. He had a warm palm and a firm, confident grip, long fingers and a big, strong hand. She was still a little overwhelmed by him. He was about six feet tall, broad shouldered, narrow hipped, lean and muscular, with buttery golden hair that waved and curled as if a woman had just run her fingers through it. Dark brows arched high above warm brown eyes that had a hint of gold in them, as if reflecting his hair. She guessed he was in his early thirties.

Wow, she thought inanely.

Eli didn't think Fiona Larkin looked like a woman who mucked out dog kennels for a living.

Far from it, he thought admiringly. She was petite and undeniably feminine. Her silken brown hair was pulled away from her pale face to lie against her neck in thick, glossy curls that gleamed in the dying sunlight streaming through the office windows. Her eyes were a heady mixture of green and blue, fringed with thick lashes and subtly enhanced with a slight touch of makeup. Her slim, curvaceous body was neatly outlined by a simple wool dress of royal blue.

Thank heaven she wasn't wearing green and red, he thought fleetingly. Much as he loved the Christmas season, *everyone* seemed to be wearing green and red this week. Then the tune of "I'll be Home for Christmas" popped into his head and he smiled happily.

"Please call me Fiona," she said.

"Eli," he supplied. He glanced inquisitively at his boss. It was nearing the end of the working day, and Arthur knew Eli's flight to Wisconsin left National Airport first thing in the morning. He wondered why he had been pulled away from his telephone conversation with his parents and suddenly called into this meeting with no prior warning.

They all sat down. Arthur opened the discussion by saying, "Eli isn't actually familiar with Oak Hill, Fiona, but he did meet Vicky Wood at a barbecue at my home."

"You mean Vicky Bennett, don't you?" Eli said.

"Of course. I met Vicky before she married, and I still tend to use her maiden name," Arthur explained to Fiona.

"You really work in Vicky Bennett's kennel?" Eli asked Fiona in some amazement. He remembered Vicky Bennett as nearly six feet tall, with an Amazon build and streaming red hair. He didn't doubt for an instant that Vicky could wrestle a Doberman pinscher to the ground, but Fiona looked too delicate for that kind of work.

"Yes. I was hired in June. Vicky made me the assistant manager after a trial period of three months."

Her voice was confident and perky, but he noticed the strain in her eyes and sensed she was too wound up to answer casual questions. His eyes dropped to her lap where her hands twisted nervously. Her hands. They were the give-away, he thought, remembering their handshake. Although elegant and finely tapered, her hands were slightly callused and rough.

Since her tension left no doubt that she was here on professional business, he asked the obvious question. "Why are you here instead of Vicky?"

"Vicky's out of town. She and Race took their baby to see Race's stepfather in California for Christmas." She looked back at Arthur. "That leaves me in charge."

"Fiona's all by herself out there at night," Arthur said with concern.

Fiona frowned suddenly. Eli guessed she didn't want to be presented as a helpless female afraid of the dark. Still, he asked, "That place is pretty far out in the country, isn't it?"

"On fifty acres at the edge of the Blue Ridge Mountains," Fiona confirmed. "But that's not the point."

"Maybe you'd better start at the beginning," Arthur advised.

"Right." Fiona pressed her palms together in front of her as she paused. For a moment, Eli thought she looked like a modern Madonna, with creamy skin, softly waving hair, delicate bone structure, prayerful posture, and a thoughtful expression on her face. How old was she anyhow, twenty-five, twenty-six?

She drew a quick breath and looked up with lively eyes. Eli forced himself to concentrate on her words instead of the smooth column of her neck or the soft sheen of her hair.

"Vicky and Race left for California three days ago. They live in the big house on the property. I live in the old care-taker's cottage. Both are separated from the actual kennel by some distance. You can hear any real commotion from my cottage, but you can't see anything because there's an oak forest in between."

She glanced anxiously at them both.

"Go on," Arthur said encouragingly.

"Well, two days ago, we couldn't find the files I had left out the night before," she said in a rush.

Eli lost the thread of her story at that point, though she was looking at him as if the implications should be obvious.

"What kind of files?" he asked at last.

"We keep complete records of all the boarders. You know, their owners' names and addresses, the dogs' names and vital statistics, medical history, services required, feeding instructions. If a dog is scheduled to be bathed or groomed before it goes home, I leave its registration form out for the groomer the night before, with all the grooming instructions printed on its chart. Then the groomer comes in around five or six o'clock in the morning to do the work so the dogs will be ready to leave as soon as we open at eight o'clock."

"I see," said Eli, wondering what this was leading to.

"So the night Vicky and Race left, I left out the files as usual. There were quite a few that night, too. More than twenty. The next morning Nadine—that's the groomer—called me at five o'clock in the morning to say she couldn't find them anywhere."

"What did you do?" asked Arthur.

"I told her where they were. She said they weren't there. I got up, got dressed, and walked over to the kennel to find them. We searched everywhere, top to bottom, but we couldn't find them."

"Maybe someone else picked them up and then misplaced them," Eli suggested reasonably. He glanced at his watch. This time tomorrow he'd be in Wisconsin with his family, he thought cheerfully.

Fiona shook her head impatiently. "Who? I—I'm trying to be extra conscientious while Vicky's gone. This is my first time running things by myself. So I actually did my paperwork around midnight that night. The last staff member leaves by ten o'clock.''

"Maybe someone came back for some reason. Did you question everyone?" Eli said.

"Yes. No one was there between the time I left and the time Nadine arrived.''

Eli frowned. "Was there any sign of forced entry?"

"No."

"Did you lock all the doors?"

"Yes."

"Are you sure every door was locked?" Eli persisted.

"Absolutely. In fact, I had only walked about a hundred yards from the kennel that night when I realized I had entered by a side door and then left by the front door. So I went back to lock the side door, and while I was there I checked all the other doors.''

"All right. Are these files valuable in some way?"

"No."

Eli glanced at Arthur. Fiona Larkin had come here, to a busy, high-powered security agency with corporate and government clients because she or her groomer had lost a few sheets of paper containing information about family pets? This was absurd. He should be on his way home to pack a suitcase instead of sitting here listening to a very pretty woman tell a very silly story.

"Well, I'm sure they'll turn up—" he began.

"How did you know?" she demanded.

"Know what?" he asked in confusion.

"They did!"

"Did what?"

"They turned up!"

"Oh," he said in bewilderment. "You found them then?"

"No."

"But you just said—"

"Yesterday morning, I discovered them exactly where I had left them two nights earlier." She seemed to be waiting for some reaction.

Gee whiz! Wow! How about that!

"Well, good...." He glanced at Arthur for help. None was forthcoming. Arthur was studying her closely.

"But don't you think that's strange?" she persisted.

"I guess so, but it happens now and then." He paused. "Is that why you came here?"

"No, of course not." This time he saw a flash of annoyance in those blue-green eyes. She took a deep breath. "I'm sorry. I'm not explaining this very well."

"You're doing just fine," said Arthur.

Like hell she is, thought Eli. I've got a load of Christmas presents I still have to wrap.

Fiona tried again. "The point is, something unusual happened. I started looking around to see if I could find anything else unusual."

"And did you?" Eli asked wearily.

"Yes. Just little things. A chair facing the wrong way, mud on the front walk—which I know had been swept clean the night before."

"Fiona, I really don't think—"

"But that's not all," she rushed on. "I've explained that you can't see the kennel from my cottage. I just had this feeling that two nights in a row someone had entered without my knowing. Last night I couldn't stop thinking about it. So finally, around midnight, I walked over there to make sure everything was okay, all the doors were locked, no one was lurking about, that kind of thing."

"And what happened?"

"Someone was lurking about."

"Really?" Now that was the first significant thing she had said.

"Yes."

"Man or woman?" asked Arthur.

"I don't know. It was dark, so I couldn't see very clearly. It was cold, so the person was covered head to foot."

"Can you guess at the height and weight?" Eli asked.

"No. He—or she—was far away when I saw him, and the clothing was bulky."

"Did you catch a glimpse of hair or skin color?"

"No."

"Can you describe the clothing in more detail?"

"No."

"Did you notice a limp or any other distinctive kind of movement?" Eli persisted.

She frowned, concentrating. "No," she said at last. "Nothing."

"Was he carrying a flashlight?"

"No."

"How far away were you?"

"I'm not sure," she said. "Maybe two hundred yards. I was just coming out of the oak grove."

"So in the middle of the night, worried about an intruder, coming out of a dark forest, you saw a dark shape two hundred yards away that you think was a prowler." Eli paused significantly before saying, "I have to ask this. Are you sure you didn't see shadows and imagine something real?"

"Yes, I'm sure!" she said desperately. "I had one of my dogs with me. As soon as we reached the edge of the grove, it stiffened and started growling. That's why I even searched the darkness instead of just walking straight ahead. I saw someone and my dog barked."

"What happened then?" Arthur asked.

"The figure jumped like it was startled and ran away."

"Your dog didn't pursue it?" Eli asked.

"My dog is . . . a little cowardly," Fiona admitted. She looked as guilty as if she had just said something disloyal about her family.

"What did you do then?" Eli persisted.

"I called the police of course. They came about a half hour later. The sheriff is a friend of Vicky's, he knows me, he keeps his K-9 dog at the kennel now and then, so he was receptive to my story," she said with a significant glance at Eli.

Eli rubbed the bridge of his nose. "Did they find any evidence of a prowler? Any footprints?"

"They found a million footprints. It's a public place. But…there was no conclusive evidence of a prowler. So the sheriff said that he really couldn't do anything more than ask a patrol car to swing by the kennel once or twice every night in case something else happens."

"Well, that seems like a very satisfactory gesture under the circumstances," Eli said reasonably.

Fiona looked at him with open exasperation. "For the next two weeks I am in sole charge of a business that belongs to someone else—Vicky and Race Bennett, to be precise, friends of Mr. Morgan here. And although no laws have been broken that enable the police to interfere, the kennel has been violated and there's a prowler lurking about."

"I don't think you—"

Fiona cut him off angrily. "These are also the busiest two weeks of the entire year for us. We're completely sold-out, every spare inch of space has an animal in it, we've hired on temporary holiday staff to pick up the extra work load, we have a lot of new customers arriving, and I'm responsible for over two hundred well-loved domestic pets. I have no way of knowing if this prowler is a practical joker who won't return, a thief, a psychopath who hates animals, or some weirdo who's eventually going to start prowling around my isolated cottage when he gets bored with the kennel! I think under the circumstances I have every reason to seek professional help!"

Her expression blazed with anger, and he had a vivid picture of the passion that lay hidden behind the lovely purity of her face. He would have admired it if he hadn't been so annoyed. "Now look, Miss Larkin—"

"Of course you have reason to seek professional help, Fiona," Arthur cut in forcibly, silencing Eli with a stern look. "I'm glad you came to us." Eli stared at him incredulously.

"You mean you'll help me?" Fiona asked weakly.

"Of course we will," Arthur assured her. Eli thought his boss was crazy, but figured he would wait until the client had left before saying so aloud.

"Oh, thank you, Mr. Morgan. I knew I could rely on you."

Fiona was studiously ignoring Eli. Well, what did he care? By this time tomorrow he'd be hugging his siblings and eating his mother's Christmas cookies.

"Henry Race was one of my closest friends," Arthur said, referring to the wealthy politician who had originally founded the kennel with Vicky and then died two years ago. "I wouldn't want to see anything happen to Oak Hill, which meant so much to him. What's more, Vicky has provided free services for my company's security dogs since opening the kennel. How could I refuse you a favor like this?"

Fiona beamed at him, relieved to have placed the problem with a professional.

"I'm sure," Arthur Morgan continued magnanimously, "that Eli can have the problem cleared up in no time."

"What?" Eli said.

"What?" Fiona said.

"Considering the importance of the relationship between our two companies, I couldn't trust this matter to anyone else than my most capable associate."

"But I have a plane—"

Arthur interrupted Eli swiftly. "He and I will discuss strategy, and he'll be there first thing in the morning, after he's had a chance to go home and pack a few belongings."

"Pack?" Fiona asked with wide eyes.

"Since your troubles seem to be occurring mainly after hours, he may need to spend a night or two there," Arthur explained.

Fiona eyed Eli as if she thought he would need a sturdy dog run to keep him out of trouble. "Well, I suppose, if it's only for a day or two..." Her tone made it clear she wasn't exactly thrilled at the prospect but felt half a loaf was better than none.

"Wait a minute," said Eli, "tomorrow morning I have to—"

"You'd better bring old clothes—something you don't mind getting stained or torn," Fiona advised Eli.

"Torn? Stained? I'm not going to get into a knife fight with anybody," Eli snapped. "In fact, I'm—"

"I mean," Fiona said with annoyance, "you'll need clothes for kennel work. Something waterproof would be best."

"Kennel work?" Things were definitely getting out of hand.

She frowned. "Well, if you're going to be hanging around all the time, I can't just tell everyone you're a private security consultant, now can I?"

"The staff are suspect, until we know more," Arthur added. "It seems best that you pose as one of them."

"But I—"

"We start work at seven o'clock in the morning, Mr. Becker. Do you think you can be there by then?"

"No! Because I'm—"

"Thank you for giving me the chance to repay Vicky some of the favors I owe her," said Arthur, rising to his feet. He kept up a steady stream of reassuring conversation as he guided Fiona to the door and assured her that Eli would be at Oak Hill bright and early the following morning.

After he closed the door behind her, he turned to face Eli. The two men regarded each other for a moment, one wary, the other radiating fury.

"I'm not doing it! It's crazy!"

"Now hear me out," said Arthur, walking slowly back to his desk.

"What's to hear? You've got a nutty—beautiful, I'll admit, but nutty—paranoid woman who freaks out the first time she's left alone in some godforsaken spot in the country and starts inventing bandits and fiends out of thin air."

"I agree the evidence is purely circumstantial—"

"What evidence? You have her word that insignificant papers were missing and then turned up again without explanation. You have a vague story of her and a cowardly dog being scared by an indistinguishable shape two hundred yards away in the dark. In short, you have nothing, Arthur. Zilch, zero, squat. There's no case here, there's just a woman who needs a baby-sitter. And I," he added between clenched teeth, "am not a baby-sitter!"

"I thought you liked her," Arthur said with a hint of mischief.

"I did until she opened her mouth."

"Nevertheless, if there's even the slightest possibility that something is wrong out there, I can't let it pass by. I owe Vicky Bennett too many favors."

"All right, all right," said Eli, raising his hands in a palms-up gesture. "If you're determined to waste agency time and money on her—" He stopped and frowned for a moment. "You still have an agreement to do jobs for Vicky Bennett for free?"

"As long as she keeps boarding the company dogs from time to time for free. I should also add that she boards my family pets for free."

"Fine, Art, if you want to go on a wild-goose chase for old times' sake and current debts, it's your agency, go ahead. But please, please, don't include me. I'm supposed to go home to Wisconsin tomorrow. This will be my first Christmas with my family in ten years."

"I know that," said Arthur sadly, "and when I asked you to quit Naval Intelligence and come to work for me, I promised you vacation time, holidays off—"

"Normally, I don't mind. But this Christmas is special, Art. My parents are counting on all of us being there together for the first time in years. We've all made a special effort to arrange it."

"I'm sure this will only take a day or two, Eli. It sounds like a simple enough case."

"Then get someone else to do it."

"I can't."

"Why not?" Eli challenged.

"Well, for one thing, it's just a few days before Christmas, so nearly everyone who isn't already on a case has left town."

"I would have, too, if I weren't finishing up the Collins report!"

"I know." There was regret in Arthur's voice.

"Bob Carter is still here. So is Naomi MacIntyre."

"Eli, I want my best man on this, and that's you," Arthur said firmly.

"Why, for God's sake?"

"Because the only other time Vicky Bennett ever came to me for help it was also a simple, quick case. I assigned one of the kids to it, and he screwed it up. Can you imagine how ashamed I felt? In letting down Vicky, I not only let down a valuable contact, but also the memory of my friend Henry Race. What's more, she forgave me for it, even though our failure resulted in her losing quite a bit of money."

Eli shifted uncomfortably in his chair. He was starting to feel trapped. Arthur pressed his advantage.

"I have more faith in you than in anyone else, Eli. That's why I spent two years talking you into coming to work for me, and that's why I want you to take care of this matter. You know that I want you to head the company when I retire." He paused, and a bleak expression crept over his face.

"This is one of those dirty jobs the boss has to do. But, Eli, I *can't* do it. I'm an old man with a bullet in my leg and a bad heart. I can't go back into the field at this stage in my life."

"Aw, Artie," said Eli helplessly. Really, what else could he do? He heaved a sigh. "All right. I'll do it. But I'm only *postponing* my ticket home, not canceling it," he warned.

Arthur Morgan beamed at him. "I'm sure you'll be home in plenty of time for Christmas turkey, Eli." He became more sober. "I want you to know how much this means to me."

"Forget it. A couple of days mucking out kennels with a crazy woman in the heart of Virginia—what man doesn't dream of that?"

Two

Eli Becker spent most of his first morning on the job in the local hospital.

"Rule number one at Oak Hill. If it doesn't wag its tail at you, don't reach out to pet it," Fiona said as she guided him toward the reception desk in the emergency room.

"Hi, Fiona! Got another live one, eh?" called a young intern as he dashed by.

"Hi, Fiona! Whadjya bring us this time?" said a nurse at reception.

"Come here often?" Eli asked Fiona suspiciously.

"It's a rough business," Fiona said.

"Workman's comp as usual, Fiona?" The receptionist didn't even wait for an answer but added, "Don't worry, I know the numbers by heart now."

The receptionist looked at Eli. Fiona saw her jaw drop, just as Nadine's had when Eli had showed up at the kennel that morning. Even dressed in old clothes and cradling his injured right arm, he looked heart-stoppingly wonderful, she admitted grudgingly.

It was in Nadine's grooming room that he had leaned over to pet a hundred-pound German shepherd and nearly lost his right hand. After seven months at Oak Hill, Fiona could tell whether or not a dog would bite just by looking at its eyes, so it had never occurred to her that Eli would be so abysmally stupid as to pet a dog that clearly didn't want to be touched.

She might be kinder to him, she might feel more compassionate toward him, if he would make even a pretense of being interested in the case or concerned about a prowler disrupting Oak Hill. But no, she fumed, he had made it absolutely clear upon arriving that morning that he still considered this a wild-goose chase and resented her wasting his time so close to Christmas.

"Hi," the receptionist said to Eli, with an adoring smile.

"Hi," Eli said, pleased to be treated like a human being after suffering Fiona's contempt on the way to the hospital. What the hell did she *mean*, you could tell by a dog's eyes if it was going to bite?

After a long pause Fiona prompted tersely, "Aren't there some papers he has to fill out?"

"Oh...yes." The receptionist handed them to Eli. "Would you mind filling out these papers?"

"I'm right-handed." Eli looked doubtfully at his stiff, throbbing right hand wrapped in a makeshift bandage.

"Here, *I'll* do it. Let's get this over with." Fiona took the papers and led him to a chair. They both sat, and she pulled a pen out of her purse and started firing off questions. "Full name?"

"Elijah Gideon Becker."

"Address."

He gave an address in Virginia, just outside the city.

"Age?"

"Thirty-four."

She scribbled silently for a few moments.

"What are you writing now?" he asked.

"How it happened." He peered over her shoulder. "Relax, I'm not writing anything derogatory."

He didn't believe her for a moment. He read her account while she wrote. He noticed she had beautiful handwriting—swirling letters and even lines. Catholic school? he wondered. Her wrist was slim and graceful as she flipped over the page and began writing on the other side.

He leaned closer and caught the subtle fragrance of her thick hair—a smell like sunshine and fresh flowers. It was the closest he had ever been to her, and the creamy smoothness of her skin still looked as flawless as a baby's, as soft as a flower petal. Did this woman really manhandle the monster that had bitten him that morning or had he imagined it?

Fiona could feel his eyes on her, searching, probing, and it unnerved her. Heat radiated from him. He slung his good arm behind her to rest on the back of her chair, and she suddenly lost her train of thought. She glanced down to where his thigh rested just inches from her own. His jeans were tight. She traced his muscles with her eyes and saw the way they bulged against the denim when he shifted slightly, and her stomach contracted. What an absurd reaction, she thought, hearing her own heartbeat in her ears.

"Twice," Eli said.

"What?" She nearly jumped out of her skin hearing his low voice so close to her ear.

"'And then bit Mr. Becker...' twice on the right hand. Before you jumped in and saved the day," he added.

She looked at him, which was a mistake. His face was very close to hers. His eyes had a strange light in them she had never seen before. Curious, soft, a little bit laughing.

"I...uh," she said. She cleared her throat. "Twice. Right." She bent over the forms and started scribbling again.

"Why didn't he bite you?" he asked musingly.

"Because I intimidated him."

Eli choked on a laugh. At five foot one, as fragile as a ballet dancer, as soft as goose down, she intimidated a dog that had attacked *him*?

She noticed his skepticism. "Vicky taught me," she explained. "I shouted angrily at him and picked him up by the scruff of the neck. That makes them feel helpless."

He frowned thoughtfully. "That's worth knowing. Especially if I'm going to be hanging around for a day or two." He took a deep breath as his injured hand suddenly throbbed painfully.

"It must hurt dreadfully," she said with the first sign of concern she'd shown for him. "Let me finish this quickly so the doctor can see you."

In the end, Eli decided, all the shots they gave him to prevent infection hurt a hell of a lot worse than being bitten. Fiona went into the examination room with him despite his protests. She always held the hand of her injured employees, she explained.

"A dog's teeth carry all kinds of nasty germs," the doctor said cheerfully.

They wrapped up his hand, pumped him full of antibiotics, prescribed some painkillers and advised him the hand would be extremely tender for a day or two.

"Now that wasn't so bad, was it?" Fiona said cheerfully as they climbed into her little economy car.

"Morgan Security is currently protecting a big multinational company's executives from death threats. I'm beginning to wish I had volunteered for the job." He sounded morose.

"Elijah Gideon Becker," she said musingly. "That's a very biblical name."

"My dad's a biblical scholar," Eli said. "Teaches courses in the Bible as history and literature at the University of

Wisconsin." He looked at her curiously. "I don't suppose you'd care to share your full name?"

She smiled. "Fiona Deirdre Mary Larkin."

"That's very Irish."

"Yeah. I never wear green. It would just be too much, y'know?"

"Do you have a big family?"

"No," she said. "Since you obviously can't do much work in the kennel in your condition, we'll have to think of something else for you to do today."

Was it his imagination or had she changed the subject quite intentionally? Well, after all, she had brought him out here to work, not to get socially acquainted.

"I think you should show me around so I know where everything is. Then, since you're certain you locked up that night, I'll search the kennel for some means of entry that you may have overlooked."

"That's a good idea. I can just tell the staff that you're investigating our structural integrity or something."

"Sure." Since he was convinced she just had an overactive imagination, he saw no need to fabricate elaborate tales for her staff, but he didn't feel like arguing again.

When they returned to Oak Hill, Fiona drove past the driveway.

"Where are you going?" Eli asked.

"Vicky and Race's house. There's a separate driveway on the other side of the property. I'll show you around there first."

She turned the car off the road and they proceeded down an oak-lined drive to a big manor house, charming for its eccentricity. It looked like a hodgepodge of different architectural styles and tastes.

"It looks like someone's been fixing up this place," he observed as they got out of the car. Various parts of the house looked decrepit while others evidenced the work of careful renovation.

"Vicky's husband, Race, has been working on it in his spare time for a couple of years. He hasn't had much time for it lately, though, what with the first baby coming, now the second one on its way, and his career being so busy. He's an architect."

Eli started walking around the house, examining doors and windows to make sure they were securely locked, looking for signs of forced entry. Fiona followed him.

"Everything looks fine here, Fiona. Do you notice anything unusual?"

"Like what?"

"Anything moved since Vicky left for California? Anything here that's not normally here?"

She looked around, trying hard to assess her surroundings. "No, it looks the same as usual to me."

"Then let's assume for the moment that if you *do* have an intruder, he hasn't been here yet. Next?"

Fiona pursed her lips at his continued belief that she had imagined the intruder, but said nothing. She led him down the path in back of the house, through the woods, and to a river. There was an old wooden footbridge across its narrowest point.

"Wow, this place is gorgeous," he said in admiration. "Even at this time of year." This late in December, the trees were bare, the grass looked bleak and gray and all the plants and flowers were dormant or dead. Nevertheless, Oak Hill moved him with its stark beauty.

"It's much more beautiful in spring, summer, and fall," Fiona said, "but if we get a good snowfall, this place looks like a postcard."

"Yes, I guess it would. Well, maybe it'll snow."

"I hope not," she said fervently. "You can't imagine how much extra work snow would make at the kennel. Especially during these next two weeks when we're filled to capacity."

"I hadn't thought of that. Have you heard the weather report lately?"

"I listen to it religiously. Slightly cloudy with a chance of snow is all they're saying. Which means nothing. It would be unusual out here to have a winter without snow," she admitted, "but I keep sending up prayers that it holds off until after New Year's Day."

They left the river behind them and continued through the trees until they reached Fiona's cottage. It was small and sturdy and cozy-looking.

"This looks inviting," Eli said.

"Yes. It's a real home," Fiona said with conviction.

As they approached the cottage, seven dogs of indeterminate breeds and varying sizes came bounding toward them, barking merrily. A quick survey assured Eli that all their tails were wagging.

"These are my dogs," Fiona explained as a furry crowd gathered around them. "Except that one. That's Rebel. She belongs to Vicky, but she's staying with me for Christmas. You can pet all of them."

"You have *six* dogs?" he asked incredulously. He didn't think her little house could hold six dogs.

"And seven cats," she added. "Now, the barn and two smaller outbuildings are about five hundred yards north of here," she pointed the way, "and to the south—"

"Wait a minute, wait a minute. Fiona, you have *thirteen* house pets?" He liked animals and his family had always had a dog while he was growing up, but he couldn't conceive of living in her little house with thirteen pets.

"Well, fourteen, actually. I have a bird, too. Mrs. Periwinkle. Do you want to see her?" Fiona asked innocently.

"I... Another time, perhaps. Listen, doesn't Vicky mind you having all these animals here?"

"Vicky? You must be kidding. Race is a little concerned, though. He's afraid he'll need to add another room onto the cottage if I keep adopting them."

"I think he's right," Eli muttered. "With six dogs, why did you take a cowardly one with you the night you went in search of a prowler?"

"I didn't honestly expect to *find* a prowler, I just wanted to make sure everything was all right. And frankly, *none* of my dogs is that reliable in a crisis."

He looked down at her dogs. Although he was a total stranger, they were whining, wagging their tails, and nuzzling him. One threw itself under his feet and lay belly-up, tripping him in an effort to get attention. He agreed with her assessment that they weren't likely to frighten off an intruder.

She was certain that nothing out of the ordinary had taken place at her cottage, so he passed it by and let her show him around the rest of Oak Hill's extensive grounds. An hour later, numb with cold and unobtrusively cradling his throbbing arm, he followed her back to the kennel.

A sweeping driveway led up to its mock Southern plantation exterior. The lobby was big and ruggedly elegant, with a stone-tiled floor and brick walls. Eli admired the rustic way it was decorated for Christmas. There was a customer speaking to the receptionist in the office, which was a separate room with a reception window connecting it to the lobby.

"Fiona! I'm glad you're back," said Ginny, the middle-aged receptionist. "Nadine said there'd been an accident."

"Yes." Fiona led Eli into the office. "Eli Becker, Ginny Murphy."

"Well, hi there!" Ginny smiled flirtatiously at him, then noticed his bandaged hand. "Got nailed, huh? Well, 'tis the season. Happens nearly every day during Christmas, with all the confusion."

Eli wished everyone wouldn't make him feel as if he was bound to get bitten again.

"Eli will be hanging around for a couple of days, Ginny. He's opening a kennel of his own and wants to, uh, study our methods under stress,'' Fiona said, ignoring Eli's facial contortions. "Help him out if he needs anything, will you?''

"You bet,'' Ginny said willingly.

"Is this your manager?'' said the forgotten customer through the reception window.

"Oh, yes, ma'am. I'm sorry I made you wait,'' Ginny said quickly. "Fiona, Mrs. Snyder has kind of a special request. I told her it was nothing to worry about, but she wants your personal guarantee.''

"What's the problem?'' Fiona asked, approaching the reception window to speak to the short, stocky, broad-faced woman.

"I'm leaving my dog with you while I go off to Hawaii for the holidays. He's been here before, and we've always been very pleased with the service.''

"Yes, I remember you now,'' said Fiona, recognition dawning. "You're the judo teacher, right?''

The woman smiled, pleased to be remembered. "That's right.''

"And your husband's a karate teacher. How is he?''

"We're getting divorced.''

"Oh, I'm sorry.''

"Don't be. *Marrying* him was the tragedy,'' the woman said acidly.

"Oh, I see,'' said Fiona. She glanced down at Eli, who had taken a seat near her. Amusement glinted in his light brown eyes.

"The problem is,'' the woman continued, "that the dog has become the real bone of contention in the divorce.''

"Uh-huh.'' Fiona looked over the counter at the fat, hairy, placid-looking dog sitting on the floor. He needed a diet, a bath, and a haircut. "That's . . . Rocky, right?''

"That's right. It's amazing how you girls remember all these dogs' names.''

"Well, some are more memorable than others,'' Fiona said tactfully.

She remembered Rocky Snyder because he was a slob. He ate like a pig, gave off noxious odors, slobbered in his water bowl, shed hair all over his inside run and made an unspeakable mess all over his outside run. She wondered if the Snyders were fighting over who had to keep Rocky. Mrs. Snyder's next comment clarified the situation.

"I've got custody of Rocky now, but I'm afraid my husband may find out he's here and try to check him out while I'm gone. I want to make sure that you won't release my little Rocky to anyone except me."

"Okay," said Fiona. Since they primarily boarded family pets, the request had never come up before. Occasionally an owner would ask a friend or employee to drive out to Oak Hill to pick up their pet for them, but no one had ever tried to take an animal without the owner's permission. "Ginny and I won't release the dog to anyone but you."

Mrs. Snyder didn't seem satisfied with that. After it became apparent that Fiona's verbal guarantee wasn't enough to reassure the woman, Fiona offered to include it as an additional clause in the regular boarding contract.

Mrs. Snyder still seemed worried that she would return from Hawaii to find her beloved Rocky had flown the coop, and it took Fiona nearly ten minutes to get her out of the lobby.

Fiona dragged a sluggish Rocky into the office with her after Mrs. Snyder had gone. "He must have a thyroid problem," she said.

Eli looked at the most unappealing dog he had ever seen. "*This* is the object of a custody battle in a divorce?"

"People can be irrational about dogs," said Fiona.

"No kidding," said Eli, thinking of the six dogs Fiona lived with in her little cottage. "A judo teacher and a karate instructor? Can you imagine what their marital squabbles must have been like?"

"They had children, too. I wonder who's got custody of them?" Fiona mused.

"If you ask me," said Ginny, "I think Mrs. Snyder's overreacting."

"So do I," said Fiona. "But if Mr. Snyder does happen to stop by, remember we've put it in the contract that we'll only release the dog to Mrs. Snyder. We're legally bound now. She could actually sue us if the dog leaves with anyone but her."

"Don't worry, it won't," said Ginny.

Fiona and Ginny spent a few minutes going over business. Although things were fairly quiet at the moment, the staff would all be flying around like acrobats by tomorrow trying to keep up with the situation, and that madness would last until early January when all the boarders finally went home.

"When is your son due back?" Fiona asked Ginny.

"Brian? He called from college two nights ago to say he wasn't sure. He's finished his exams, but he's still got an overdue term paper to finish. His professor has given him an extended deadline of Christmas Eve, but if it's not in by then he'll give Brian an Incomplete. I told Brian what I'd do if I had to pay for the course again just because he didn't hand in his paper on time." Ginny nodded emphatically. "He'll finish it."

Fiona sighed. As exasperating as Brian was, he was an experienced employee. Knowing his tendency to procrastinate, especially where schoolwork was concerned, she now assumed she couldn't count on him to turn up until after Christmas Eve.

"Anything else?" she asked.

"Vicky called again."

"That's the twelfth time," said Fiona. "She's supposed to be on vacation."

Ginny grinned. "Race caught her at it this time. He took the phone away from her and told me she won't be calling again. This is her first vacation since he married her and she's going to enjoy it if it kills her."

"Good," said Fiona emphatically. "The whole reason she hired me was to take some of the burden off her shoulders."

Fiona had hoped that Eli could enter the scene without attracting too much attention, but as she introduced him around the kennel it became clear that he would be the focus of everyone's fascination as long as he remained.

"Don't you have any men working for you?" he asked after she had introduced him to everyone currently on duty.

"No. Twenty women, no men."

"Why not?"

"A lot of reasons. Women are generally better with dogs and cats than men are. A lot of the staff are college kids, and the girls are more reliable than boys. And not that many men apply for work here."

But Fiona knew the girls weren't staring at him just because he was a man. After all, they had dozens of male customers every day at Oak Hill. It was because Eli, even at first glance, was such an unusual man.

His physical prowess was obvious, especially in those tight jeans which outlined his body so enticingly that a healthy woman's imagination couldn't help but fill in the details. The rolled up sleeves of his flannel shirt revealed strong forearms with a light dusting of golden hair that would softly tickle a woman's skin. His height and the breadth of his powerful shoulders made Fiona feel protected and threatened by turns when he stood near her.

However, although she'd known him for less than twenty-four hours, Fiona had already realized that his appeal ran deeper than his good looks. He had intelligent, searching eyes, trained to absorb every detail of his surroundings. She noticed that he assessed people and situations quickly and incisively. He moved with efficient grace, like a man who had trained his body to do exactly what he required of it. He had an air of strength and integrity. He even, she was forced to admit, had a reasonably good sense of humor.

Fiona assumed he lived alone, since he was obviously planning to fly home alone for his family Christmas. She wondered if he had always lived by himself. She wondered if he saw a particular woman or many women. She wondered why she was wondering about his private life.

"I wish you hadn't told everyone I'm opening a kennel of my own," he told her later.

"I had to tell them something. And they know we don't hire many men."

"If you must lie, Fiona, it's safer to tell a story that's at least fairly close to the truth. If anyone asks me about my 'plans,' they'll realize instantly I don't know the first thing about kennels."

"Then they'll assume that's why you're spending so much time here. Now let's begin your education." She turned her back on him, aware that he wanted to continue arguing.

She showed him around the kennel, explaining things as they went: the gift shop where they sold not only pet supplies, but also crafts with a canine theme; the kitchen where they prepared food and medications for their boarders; the elegant lounge where local animal interest groups met; the staff room; the cat room; the food storage room.

"Five thousand pounds of dog food?" Eli said in awe.

"Yes. I'd better order more if I don't want to run out," Fiona said with a thoughtful frown. "Come on, I'll show you the main event."

"What's that?"

"Our two hundred indoor-outdoor dog runs."

She showed him how the major portion of the kennel was divided into four separate wings, each consisting of fifty indoor-outdoor runs of varying sizes to accommodate all breeds of dogs.

Eli was impressed by how spotlessly clean the entire kennel was—certainly cleaner than his office back at the agency.

Later in the day he realized why it was clean when he saw Fiona inspect everything and then politely but firmly insist one worker redo a job that wasn't done to her satisfaction. To gain the girl's cooperation, Fiona shared the task evenly with her, tactfully offering suggestions about how to do the job better and more thoroughly.

Works well with others, Eli thought wryly. He wondered what Fiona was like when she played. There were brief glimpses of a fun woman underneath the worry, fatigue, strain, tension, and ill-temper caused by her current situation.

Trying to be as unobtrusive as possible, he spent the day inspecting the kennel, looking for signs of forced entry that Fiona may have missed, looking for means of ingress that she may have overlooked. He considered it a waste of time, but professional integrity made him do the job as thoroughly as if the kennel were the White House.

From time to time during the day he encountered Fiona, always working like a demon. He could see that this job meant a lot to her, and he supposed that was what had led her to taking such extreme measures—approaching Morgan Security—over such insubstantial worries. He knew she was tired; it was so apparent in her face. Until now he had attributed it to nerves and an overactive imagination keeping her awake at night. But if she had also been working this hard every day, it was a miracle she wasn't dead on her feet.

Every time he saw her, she was doing hard physical labor, organizing her staff to prepare for the enormous influx of boarders they expected the following day, dealing with customers who had elaborate requests, handing out Christmas cookies and eggnog to the various delivery men, repairmen, and handymen who stopped by, wrestling with dogs that certainly outweighed her, or going over staff schedules, supply lists, and financial accounts. Just watching her exhausted Eli.

Since the kennel was enormous, it was dark out by the time he completed his inspection. He approached Fiona, who was sitting in the staff room with a sad-looking cocker spaniel.

"He won't eat," she said worriedly. "I've tried everything. I poured hot beef broth over his food, I bought him a carryout hamburger, I've offered him cheese, breakfast cereal, egg rolls. I thought if I sat here with him in the quiet for a while it might make him eat. Nothing works."

"What's wrong with him?" Eli asked to be polite.

"He feels abandoned." She looked up at him.

Eli was stunned by the distress he saw in her aqua-colored eyes. She was suffering as much as the dog. "Abandoned?"

"His family left him here two days ago, and he has no way of knowing they're coming back right after Christmas. He misses them. He's afraid they've left him for good."

She was in control of herself, but her voice sounded so desolate that Eli had a wild urge to scoop her and the dog up in his arms and comfort them both. The dog sat hunched on the floor with a miserable, forlorn look in its big brown eyes. Fiona petted him and tried to tempt him with some food. He turned away.

Fiona sighed and shook her head. "He hasn't eaten since he arrived."

"How long can they keep this up?"

"A long time," she said wearily. Her eyes searched his face. "Did you want to see me about something?"

He wanted to smooth her rumpled hair away from her face and cradle her in his arms. She looked so sad and exhausted, so small and fragile, it squeezed his insides. "There's no sign of forced entry anywhere. All your doors and windows are secure."

"You mean you're convinced no one came here in the middle of the night?"

"It's theoretically possible. This place was obviously built to keep dogs in rather than to keep people out. In terms of security, it's as leaky as a sieve."

Fiona's eyes widened with alarm.

"However," he continued, "most means of entry would require considerable effort. Since nothing has been stolen or vandalized, I suggest that if there was an intruder, it was someone with a key."

"Oh." Fiona turned away from him with a worried expression.

He watched her closely, wondering what she was thinking. "How many people have keys to this building?"

"Um . . . a lot," she said hesitantly.

"Your staff members?"

"Yes." Her voice was so soft he had trouble hearing her.

"All your staff members, even temporary holiday help?"

She nodded. "So they can get in to work if they're scheduled before our office hours, and so they can lock up if they're scheduled on the late shift."

"Well, that's it then," he said. "If you're sure some-one's letting themselves in here at night, we'll just keep a close eye on some of those college kids you hired just for the holiday period. Perhaps we should even consider confiscating their keys."

She nodded distractedly. He was a little exasperated that she hadn't thought of that herself, but he reasoned that she was overwrought.

"Fiona? Is there anyone you... What's wrong?" She was looking at him with a stricken expression.

"We haven't . . . Vicky told me we haven't had the locks changed since the kennel was built."

He frowned. "And?"

"We have a *lot* of staff wandering through here, Eli. College kids, high school kids, grown women who work here for a while then go on to something else. The winter months are so slow that we only employ half the staff year-round.''

"What's your point?"

"Well, we give keys to everyone who works for us."

He stared at her. "Are you trying to tell me you don't get those keys back?"

"Not always," she admitted weakly.

"Do you mean to say," he said incredulously, "that there are dozens of ex-employees wandering around out there with keys to your business?"

"Well, *sometimes* we get them back," she said, as if trying to make amends.

"Did you tell this to the police?"

"No, I didn't think of it at the time."

"You didn't think of it?" he snapped. "A five-year-old child could have thought of that, Fiona! I just spent an entire day inspecting every inch of this damn kennel instead of flying home to my family because you simply *forgot* that half the county has keys to this place?"

"I have a lot on my mind!"

"Why the hell have you people never bothered to collect keys from ex-employees?"

"Because we didn't think it was necessary! Who would break into a kennel? Where would you be more likely to get caught than in a building filled with two hundred dogs? And anyhow, we don't keep anything valuable here!"

"Nothing?"

"Nothing!"

"Money?"

She stopped and stared at him. "Well...yes, there is some money here," she admitted more quietly.

"Has it occurred to you that most people consider money valuable?" he said in exasperation.

She sat down, feeling deflated. "I make a bank deposit every day. We keep very little cash here overnight. Not nearly enough for someone to risk arrest."

"Fiona, people have committed murder for less than a dollar."

"We post signs saying the property is patrolled by guard dogs," she added hopefully.

"And is it?"

"No."

"And does everyone who's ever worked for you *know* that it's not patrolled by guard dogs?"

"Yes."

He threw his hands up. "This is absurd. If there was anyone out there that night—"

"If? There was! I saw him!"

He considered shaking her till her teeth rattled, but he opted for civilized discussion instead. "All right. The obvious thing to do, Fiona, is to call a locksmith, have him come out first thing in the morning and change all the locks. Then we will only issue keys to your most reliable employees. It is entirely possible that that will be the end of the matter. Agreed?"

His patronizing tone made her clench her teeth, but she agreed. Had she honestly thought this man was at all likable? He was pompous, bossy, pushy, unreasonable and rude.

"And you're making the dog nervous!" she snapped as an afterthought.

Eli closed his eyes and appeared to be counting to ten. When he opened them again he looked as if the experience hadn't helped to calm him at all.

"I'm going out to get some dinner now, Fiona. I'll come back around ten o'clock, and then you can show me where to bed down. Tomorrow we'll call the locksmith and arrange for him to come do a job that should have been done

before you called in a security expert—particularly before
you called *me* in, the night before I was supposed to fly
home to my family.''

With that parting shot, he stalked out the door before Fiona could think of a suitably acerbic comeback.

Three

———

Fiona locked up the kennel herself that night and checked three times to make sure everything was secure. She was *not* going to put up with her smart-aleck security expert lecturing her again.

By the time she had carried sheets, blankets and a pillow from her cottage to the kennel, her natural fairness of mind had begun to make her feel guilty about the way she had acted earlier.

He had a point. There was no denying that. She should indeed have changed all the locks on the doors before calling Morgan's. But she was a kennel manager, not a security expert. She dealt with dogs and people, feeding supplies and bank deposits, sanitation and public relations. She knew nothing about security, means of entry and deductive reasoning.

She wasn't accustomed to thinking in those terms, so naturally she would be a little slow on the uptake. After all, Eli was equally a novice in her field—he'd managed to get himself bitten his first five minutes on the job. So while he had a point, he had no reason to be so snappish about it.

Well, actually he *did*, she acknowledged as she let herself back into the kennel with her enormous bundle of bedding. He had expected to be home for Christmas with his family, and instead he was here staking out a dog kennel.

She hated Christmas. More than any other annual event, Christmas reminded Fiona of how alone in the world she was. Even her fourteen house pets couldn't remove the chill that was creeping into her heart as Christmas Day crept inexorably closer.

She took a quick steadying breath after she dropped her cumbersome bundle on top of a couch in the lounge. Then she went into the kitchen to make a pot of coffee. She supposed Eli would want something to keep him awake for his stakeout, and she needed to keep busy while she contemplated apologizing to him.

Although Christmas in Fiona's life was just something to get through as quickly and as painlessly as possible, she understood that it meant more to millions of people. Eli was obviously one of them, and until she could prove that she hadn't ruined his Christmas for a wild-goose chase, he was going to be a little testy. She had already observed that patience with people wasn't one of his strong points.

She filled her favorite mug—a birthday gift from Nadine—with coffee and sighed. She would obviously have to swallow her pride and apologize to Eli. She had been guilty of a very obvious oversight, and she should have shown more humility when he had pointed it out to her today.

And if *he* wanted to apologize for his disproportionate annoyance with her, well, they could talk about that, too.

Eli let himself into the kennel with his own key just after ten o'clock that night. He smelled brewing coffee and followed the aroma into the kitchen. He smiled. Fiona had made a fresh pot for him.

His mind filled with an image of her as he had last seen her; proud and defensive, her sea-colored eyes flashing at him, her pale cheeks flushed with anger, her shapely body camouflaged beneath layers of warm work clothes that still couldn't hide her fragility. He had actually found himself feeling guilty about yelling at her, although she was certainly not meek or defenseless.

He started looking around the darkened, shadowy kennel for her. The dogs were bedded down for the night. They were fairly quiet except for some mournful howling. No wonder Fiona was jumpy. That sound could play tricks on your nerves.

He finally found her in the lounge. She had her back to the door and was struggling with a quilt.

"What are you doing?" he asked.

"Yahh!" She nearly hit the ceiling. She whirled to face him and pressed a hand to her heaving bosom, very clearly outlined beneath the long woolen underwear she was wearing. "You scared me out of ten years' growth!"

"I'm sorry," he said. He meant it. The kennel did seem pretty spooky at night—dark, isolated and haunted by faint, forlorn wailing coming from the four wings housing dogs.

"It's okay," she said, recovering her breath. "I didn't realize anyone was here." She shivered involuntarily. It was frightening to think she could be in the kennel and not realize that someone else was there with her. Thoughts like these had never disturbed her before, and she had never considered the kennel anything but a friendly, welcoming place.

Eli noticed her shiver and came closer, wanting to comfort her. "It's pretty eerie in here at night."

Her eyes thanked him for not making fun of her. She had shed layers of clothing here in the warm lounge. He noticed for the first time that for all her apparent fragility, she had some pretty good muscle development. Drawn by an irresistible urge to touch her, he laid his hands on her upper arms and gently squeezed.

"Where'd you get those?"

"What?" she asked. Her voice was a little breathless again.

"Muscles."

She was startled and more than a little unbalanced by the sudden warmth in his eyes and the gentleness of his touch. "I . . . uh, hard work. I mean, I work hard."

"I noticed. You're a dynamo. Every time I turned around today, you were picking up something bigger than yourself." His hands moved to her shoulders. "It feels like all of you is pretty strong." He squeezed gently again and raised his brows in surprise. "You're tense."

"Is it any wonder?" she said weakly. She was afraid she'd start trembling. Surely he didn't mean to get her this excited. Surely she would just embarrass them both if she collapsed into a passionate little puddle at his feet the way she wanted to.

With skillful, knowing hands, with hands that must have explored many women to be so clever, he started massaging her shoulders and neck, letting his gaze travel over her tired face as he did so.

"Maybe this will help," he murmured.

His left hand kneaded and probed while his injured right hand petted and stroked. Fiona groaned involuntarily as she felt warmth spread from those soothing, strong hands and ooze through her body with delicious languor.

"Relax," he whispered into her hair.

She let her head tilt forward to rest against his chest. She could feel how broad and warm and hard he was. She figured he must have more muscle in his chest than she had in her whole body. His body had a tantalizing aura of power and strength that made her feel giddy. Unless it was the massage making her feel giddy. Or the way he was nuzzling her hair. She started to tremble.

"They say we carry anger and fear between our shoulder blades," he said as his magic hands started probing that area. "I know what you're afraid of. Are you still angry at me?"

"Actually," she said, her voice muffled against his chest, "that's what I wanted to talk to you about."

"Oh?"

"Yes." She pulled back to look into his face. Her eyes were very serious. Then her gaze dropped to his mouth.

Fiona suddenly pulled away from him. She couldn't concentrate while standing so close to him, pressed so firmly against him that he must surely feel the way her nipples were hardening into tight buds. This is crazy, she thought.

"I, uh, wanted to apologize. You know, for the locks and the keys and everything. I should have thought of that before I called you, but . . ." She shrugged.

"I know you've had a lot on your hands since Vicky left," he said, accepting her apology gracefully. He should have stopped there. "We'll get the locks changed, and that should put your mind to rest."

Fiona frowned. She picked up a quilt and started trying to spread it evenly over the couch, which she had done her best to make into a comfortable bed.

"Changing the locks won't explain to me why someone stole some files and then returned them, or why someone is lurking around here," she said evenly.

He sighed expressively. Her eyes flashed up to his face. She decided not to pick another fight with him. Instead she smiled challengingly and said, "Before you leave here, Eli Becker, you're going to grovel in mortification for not believing me from the start."

"We'll see," he said. She was proud, all right, but he liked the way it made her eyes glow. He wouldn't argue with her anymore tonight.

After another moment he watched as she straightened and surveyed her handiwork. Her long underwear looked like a sturdy, practical brand. He wondered if any other woman could look so seductive in it.

"I hope this will be comfortable enough," she said, eyeing the makeshift bed uncertainly.

"It's fine," he assured her.

"The kids almost never come in here. As long as you're up by seven o'clock and store your bedding in that closet over there, they'll probably never even know you're staying here. You can shower in Nadine's room."

"That shower she uses for bigger dogs?" he asked dubiously.

"That's right. Don't worry. It's cleaner than the showers in most people's homes." She looked around. "Well, do you need anything else?" she asked at last.

About five foot one of woman, wrapped in the latest style of waffle-weave underwear, he wanted to say. "No, thanks."

They stood staring at each other. It suddenly seemed intimate to him that she had made his bed. He wanted to hold her again, wanted to feel the firmness of her warm body under his hand, the softness of her chestnut hair against his face, the delicate torture he had felt with the peaks of her nipples burning into his chest. He wanted to caress her, to feel her skin under that underwear, to pull her down into the bed she had made for him with her slim, work-hardened hands....

"Well, good night then," she said softly.

"Good night." He watched as she started to leave, feeling bereft. "Hey, do you want me to walk you home?" he asked suddenly.

She glanced doubtfully out at the dark night through the window. Then her eyes took on the proud glitter he was already coming to recognize. "No, thanks. I'll be fine."

She obviously didn't want to be taken for a silly female afraid of the dark. He wished for a long time after her departure that she would have let him walk her home. He recognized, with annoyance, that his motives weren't entirely gallant.

Knock it off, Becker, you're supposed to be working.

His right arm was throbbing painfully and his fingers were stiff, but he didn't want to take a painkiller for fear it would make him drowsy. He didn't believe for a moment that Fiona's phantom prowler would turn up, but it was too deeply ingrained in him to be alert on the job. He settled down with a spy novel and kept his ears open for a burglar who would never show up.

After a tense but uneventful walk through the woods, Fiona arrived at her little cottage. She was just about to enter when she had heard a car door slam. Since everything sounded suspicious to her these days, she turned away from the front door where her dogs eagerly awaited her and crept down to the riverbank in the dark. She crouched there for several moments, paralyzed by fear. She didn't care how ridiculous Eli Becker thought this all was; every instinct she possessed told her that something was terribly wrong at Oak Hill.

She was debating whether or not to cross the river. It was another very dark night, but she was still afraid of exposing herself to view on the bridge. She strained her ears but heard no other unusual sounds.

She was just setting her foot on the bridge when she saw a beam of light pierce the night. She gasped and dropped to the cold ground. She kept her eyes riveted on the house. The light was darting around, searching.

With her heart pounding in her chest and her breath roaring in her ears, she ran to the trees in a low crouch and then raced back to her house. She locked the door and grabbed the telephone.

Of course her security expert *would* be on the other side of the property from the manor house. Why did things never go the way you planned them? She dialed the kennel number with numb fingers.

When the telephone rang at midnight, Eli stared at it, wondering who would be calling now. If it was a customer, he couldn't help them. If it was Fiona's prowler, he didn't want anyone to know he was here. But if it was Fiona checking on him, he would only worry her by not answering. Eli picked up the receiver on the eighth ring and put it to his ear.

Fiona heard no reassuring "hello?" or identifiable voice. Just a deadly silence. Terror clutched her chest. It took her a moment to realize she was panting. She forced herself to confront the person on the other end of the line. "Who's that?"

"Fiona?" Eli said, recognizing her voice. It was laced with fear. "It's me. What's wrong?"

"There's someone prowling around Vicky's house," she whispered. "I didn't imagine him. He's got a flashlight this time."

Fiona's house was just a short distance from Vicky's, and she was alone there with her useless dogs. Fear ran cold through Eli's veins.

"Don't leave your house. I'll be right there."

After she hung up, Fiona breathed a sigh of relief. Then she wondered why the hell Eli couldn't answer the phone like a normal person? All she had to do now was sit tight and wait. He had long legs, surely he could run fast.

"He'll be here in no time," she told her dogs. They ignored her. She picked up Tidbit, the smallest dog, and clutched her to her chest for comfort. Tidbit yelped in protest. "Sorry," she said, loosening her death grip on the dog.

She was pacing the floor with Tidbit in her arms when Vicky's dog, Rebel, suddenly tensed and started to growl. Fiona's dogs immediately followed suit and either stood glassy-eyed and growling or cowered at Fiona's feet.

Someone was out there, she realized. Who was it? Trying to figure out how she could identify Eli without actually opening her door, she backed out of the well-lit living room and into her darkened bedroom.

She glanced out the window and gasped when she saw the beam of a flashlight approaching the cottage. She slid out of view as it passed by her window.

She heard a small voice—thin, wispy, repetitive—and realized with a weird sense of detachment that it was her own. "Ohmigod, ohmigod, Eli, Eli, Eli, ohmigod."

There was a soft knock on her front door.

"Shut up," she ordered herself.

All of her dogs had followed her into the bedroom, and she realized that her tension and terror were frightening them. Their growling and whimpering scraped along her nerves.

The knocking stopped. She waited to see what would happen next.

Then she saw the door handle twisting and turning as someone tried to gain entry to her house. The door was locked, but her cottage was hardly a fortress. If someone really wanted to enter, it wouldn't take him long to force his way in.

She was so scared she just wanted to dissolve into a puddle and cry. Instead, she looked around the bedroom for something she could use to defend herself.

Eli blamed himself. Had he ever once taken this whole thing seriously? Had he even stopped to consider that if an ex-employee was prowling around at night, it could well be a very unbalanced person intent on harming Fiona? No, all he had thought about was wrapping this up as quickly as possible so he could go home for Christmas.

The cold air stung his nostrils and burned his heaving chest as Eli ran through the dark night faster than he had ever run in his life. She was alone out there with some man-

iac prowling around, and he'd never forgive himself if anything happened to her. How could he have been so
stubborn, selfish and stupid?

He tripped on a root and flew head over heels to land with
a crashing thud against a tree. He shook his head, dazed and
winded, groaning as his bitten right hand shot pain through
his whole arm.

He dragged himself to his feet and continued running,
trying to be more careful this time, trying to control the
panic sweeping through him. He knew better than to let his
emotions interfere in a dangerous situation. He'd be of no
help to Fiona if he didn't force himself to think clearly and
coldly.

He could see the glow from her windows as he neared the
cottage, and it reassured him.

Fifty yards later, still running like a madman, he saw the
large bulky figure of Fiona's nightmares testing the knob on
her front door.

Eli bared his teeth in a silent snarl and rushed forward. He
would kill the man before he'd let him hurt her.

Fiona was clutching an umbrella in her shaking hands,
wondering if it would work as a weapon, when all hell broke
loose.

She heard a roar of rage outside the house, an incoherent
shout, and then a series of thuds, like two heavy objects
colliding again and again. Six of the dogs ran into the living room and starting barking uproariously. The seventh,
the biggest, hid under the bed.

Shock and surprise made Fiona forget her fear. She
dropped her umbrella and followed the crowd into the living room. They were all hurtling themselves at the doors and
windows. She ran to a window and looked out.

All she could see at first was a rolling, twisting, dark
shape moving around on the ground outside her cottage.
She turned on the porch light, but it was old and dim and

added only a little illumination to the bodies rolling toward the trees. Nevertheless, she could make out white checkered squares which she recognized as Eli's flannel shirt.

Eli! He had arrived in time to save her!

His assailant was wearing dark, bulky clothing and a knit cap, so she still had no hope of identifying the stranger. She ran from window to window, tripping over excited dogs and following the two men with her eyes as they scrambled around with their hands at each other's throats. She had no doubt that the prowler was a man, since even Vicky Bennett couldn't have fought so ferociously against Eli's attack.

Eli threw the other man off him and jumped to his feet. As the other man stood, Eli slugged him with his right fist. The other man fell down again, but rather than continue the attack, Eli howled and jumped around, clutching his injured right hand in agony.

Fiona shook her head. "Should've used the left, dummy."

The other man apparently realized that Eli's right hand was useless to him now. He clambered to his feet, and renewed his attack. He tried several punches which Eli, still clutching his right hand, dodged without raising an arm. Finally, tiring of this, the stranger launched a flying tackle against Eli and knocked him to the ground. At that point the attacker's cap flew off, revealing blond hair a few shades paler than Eli's. The two men went tumbling into a mud puddle, and within moments they were indistinguishable from each other in Fiona's eyes.

Realizing that Eli might not subdue his opponent now that he had managed to completely disable his right arm, Fiona decided he needed help. She grabbed a cast-iron skillet from her kitchen and ran out the front door. Her dogs followed close behind, running around the yard, barking, howling and wagging their tails as if this were all a new game invented for their benefit.

Fiona rushed over to where the two bodies struggled in the dark, hoping she could influence the outcome of the fight. But finding them intertwined as they were, two muddy blond men of about the same size, Fiona couldn't quite make out which was which. She decided to try them from the other side. She gingerly stepped around their struggling, thrashing, cursing bodies. Without warning they burst into a sudden flurry of movement and rolled toward her violently.

Fiona gasped as their combined weight and velocity propelled her backward with such force she fell over a bush and crash-landed in its thorns. By the time she extracted herself, shoved her dogs out of the way, and found her frying pan, the two men had scuffled and scrambled their way across the yard.

That does it!

She ran toward them with renewed determination. One of them sat up and pulled the other to a sitting position, apparently just to knock him down again. Fiona raised the skillet over her head with deadly intent. They both looked up as her form blocked out the porch light.

"No!" they screamed in unison.

"But someone's got to help you!" she cried.

"I don't want help!" Eli snarled.

"Are you *nuts*?" shouted the other man. Eli slugged him with his left fist. Then the two of them were at it again.

Men, Fiona thought with disgust. Eli clearly didn't want her help, but she really didn't think she could just stand around and watch him get beaten to a pulp. She clutched her frying pan and tried to decide what to do next as Tidbit tugged at her ankle.

"Go inside!" Eli shouted.

"Call the police!" cried the other man.

"What?" said Eli.

"What?" said Fiona.

"Get the sheriff! Get the cops! Go to the phone for God's sake! What's the *matter* with you?" the stranger continued hysterically.

Those words, that voice, that blond hair. "Oh, no," said Fiona slowly.

Eli shook the other man by the scruff of the neck and dragged him closer to the porch light. "Who the hell are you?" he snarled.

Fiona ran over to the two of them and peered at the stranger. A familiar pair of pale blue eyes peered back at her.

"What the hell is going on here?" he asked wildly.

"Brian! What are *you* doing here?" Fiona exclaimed.

"You *know* him?" Eli demanded.

"Of course! Let go of him!" Fiona tried to prise Eli's hands off of Brian's neck.

"Who the hell is he?" Eli and Brian demanded at the same time.

"You're choking him!" Fiona said.

"Why was he trying to break into your house in the middle of the night?" Eli punctuated each word by shaking Brian. Brian's blond hair flopped about, and his eyes started to roll back in his head.

"I think I'm going to faint," he gasped weakly.

With a disgusted grunt, Eli released him. Brian slid to the ground in a big, muddy heap. Fiona dropped to her knees and cradled his head.

"Brian!" She looked accusingly up at Eli. "Now look what you've done!"

"I was trying to *help* you! You call me in a panic in the middle of the night because you've seen your phantom prowler again, and when I get here I find this hulk trying to break into your house! What did you expect me to do?"

Since she had expected him to do exactly what he did, she supposed she'd better stop complaining. "I'm sorry. I'm overwrought."

"No kidding!" He wiped some mud off his face and held his pain-racked right arm. "So am I."

Fiona shook Brian experimentally. There was no reaction. "Can you revive him?"

Eli glanced down at the recumbent form next to Fiona. "Get up or I'll kick you from here to eternity."

Brian groaned and rolled to a sitting position.

"Works every time," said Eli. "Now who the hell are you?"

"I've told you. That's Brian. He works here," said Fiona.

"He *works* here?"

"Well, it's probably more accurate to say he collects his pay here," Fiona admitted.

"Hey! I resent that! I've given the best years of my life to this place," Brian protested as he hauled himself painfully to his feet.

"You told me you don't have any men working for you," Eli said to Fiona.

"I don't," she replied.

"Hey!" said Brian.

"He's just a kid," Fiona said by way of explanation.

"Fiona, he outweighs me by thirty pounds," Eli snapped.

"He's a football player at college."

"This is getting us nowhere," Eli said grumpily.

"Get off me!" Brian snarled as three of Fiona's dogs finally recognized him and started slobbering on him.

"Maybe we should all go inside and calm down for a moment," Fiona suggested.

They moved into the house and she spread some old blankets over the furniture for her two mud-covered guests and made a pot of coffee. Eli looked as if he would gladly finish thrashing Brian, who held his aching head in his hands and rocked back and forth.

Eli was stunned and furious by turns as he reviewed recent events. He was astonished by his unprofessional emotionalism the moment he had thought Fiona was in danger, outraged that she had scared him for no reason and shocked at how relieved he was that she was safe. He could kill her young employee for being the cause of all this. He tried to move the fingers of his right hand and grunted when pain shot through his arm. Why had destiny sentenced him to getting tangled up with this crazy woman and her blasted boarding kennel?

"All right," he said, taking charge of the situation after Fiona had poured them all some hot coffee. "Let's start with the obvious question. Why were you prowling around here in the middle of the night?"

"Who *is* this guy?" Brian asked Fiona.

"He's... He's...um... It's hard to explain," Fiona said. "Just answer him for now."

"I came to see Vicky."

"She's not here. Didn't your mom tell you that?" Fiona said.

"I haven't seen Mom yet," Brian admitted. "She doesn't know I'm home. I wanted to see Vicky first."

"Why?" Eli asked tersely.

"I, uh, stretched the truth about something on the phone. There's a class I told Mom I might get an Incomplete in, but in fact I've flunked it."

Fiona gasped. "Brian, why did you lie like that?"

"I was just trying to prepare her for the inevitable, Fiona," Brian said defensively. "Mom's getting older. You've got to break bad news to her gently."

"Oh, really, Brian," Fiona said irritably.

"So why were you at Vicky's?" Eli persisted.

"Mom looks up to Vicky at lot. I thought Vicky could tell her for me. You know, make her see reason." He paused. "Because she was kind of unreasonable when I tried to break it to her gently."

"That doesn't explain why you were prowling around Vicky's house with a flashlight," Eli said.

"Hey, man, it's four days before Christmas and the house was completely dark and the car was gone. Like, Vicky *never* goes away, especially not just before the holidays. I was trying to figure out what was wrong."

Eli shoved a cat off his lap and stood up. "So then you came down to Fiona's house to ask where Vicky was."

"That's right. And the lights were on, but she didn't answer when I knocked. So I figured she was in the shower, or maybe out for a walk with some of her monsters. And since it's pretty cold tonight, I wanted to wait for her inside. I mean, I can't go home till I figure out what to tell Mom." He frowned briefly. "But I was really surprised that the door was locked, because Fiona never locks her door."

Eli believed him. Partially because it was a plausible story and partially because Fiona, who was scowling by now, so clearly believed him. He felt stiff, battered and exhausted. He watched Fiona curl up in her easy chair and suddenly wanted nothing so much as to curl up there with her and fall asleep.

Tidbit, two other dogs and a cat all climbed up on Brian's chair and started vying for his attention. He looked at Fiona in exasperation. "How many more of these mutts are you going to adopt, Fiona? Don't you think it's getting a little out of hand?"

She shrugged helplessly. "What else can I do? They were abandoned."

Eli looked at her sharply. "All these . . . these creatures were abandoned?" She nodded. "So you adopted them." His eyes stayed on her, curious, speculative, and she started to flush.

"Look, I've told you what *I'm* doing here," Brian said. "Now can you tell me why you attacked me like a kamikaze Sherman tank?"

Eli caught Fiona's questioning gaze. They could easily lie to Brian, but he might be clever enough to be suspicious. Anyhow, Brian might be a good backup; the kid could take a lot of punishment. Eli nodded to Fiona, indicating she could tell the truth.

Fiona explained her worries to Brian, the strange incidents that had led her first to the police and then to Morgan Security Inc.

"Morgan?" Brian said with a frown. "Aren't those the same guys that screwed up last time Vicky used them?"

"What?" said Fiona. Her worried eyes searched Eli's face.

"Yeah," Brian said, looking at Eli assessingly. "Some deadbeat owed us a few thousand bucks for boarding. When Vicky realized he intended to abandon the dogs and stick us with the bill, she called Morgan. They guy disappeared, and they never found him. Vicky lost a few grand and had to find homes for the dogs."

"When did this happen?" Fiona asked.

"About a year and a half ago," Brian said.

"Is this true?" Fiona asked Eli quietly.

He shrugged. "I've only been at Morgan since early this year. Arthur did say, however, that Morgan had failed its first assignment for Vicky."

"Are you sure you want to give these guys another chance, Fiona?" Brian asked as he massaged his tender jaw.

Fiona watched Eli with darkening aqua eyes. "It seems that no one at your agency ever takes us very seriously, Mr. Becker."

Under Fiona's accusing gaze, Eli felt as guilty as Brian had looked when explaining his subterfuge about his grades. He was uncomfortably aware that he had failed to behave with appropriately professional conduct on this case. He had openly refused to take the client's case seriously because she had no evidence of real disturbance, because she had approached Morgan's since she knew they would handle the matter for free and because he wanted to go home for Christmas.

Not only that, but he was becoming inappropriately interested in the client—who was currently looking at him as if he were a suspect piece of meat. He heaved a sigh and resolved to remedy all of these errors—especially the last one.

"Look, Fiona, why don't we all turn in, get a good night's sleep, and start fresh in the morning? Then we can—"

"I'm not paying you to sleep," she said coldly.

"You're not paying me at all!" he snapped, already forgetting his good intentions. She was a maddening woman!

"Nevertheless, while you've been bumbling around here, someone has had ample time to break into the kennel again. I suggest you go back and hunt for clues."

"'Hunt for clues'?" he repeated incredulously. "You've been watching too much TV, Fiona."

"I like that idea about hitting the sack," Brian piped up.

"Shut up," Eli and Fiona said in unison.

"Don't talk to him like that," Fiona snapped at Eli.

The complete unfairness of that remark made Eli choke on his outrage.

"You go home and explain to your mother what you just told me," Fiona ordered Brian.

"Aw, Fifi." Brian tried to look pathetic.

"It won't work," she told him. "And *don't* call me Fifi. Now leave. Out. Split. Am-scray. And Vicky would tell you the same thing."

Brian squirmed, looking for an excuse to avoid the inevitable. "Maybe I'd better help your private eye here look for clues or bad guys or something."

Eli winced. "Thanks, but I'll bumble along without your help tonight, kid."

Fiona stood up decisively and opened the door for Brian. He left reluctantly, giving one last theatrical groan when she told him to be at work bright and early the following morning.

Eli stood up to leave, too. Now that Fiona had actually managed to go two whole sentences without insulting him, Eli was feeling a little guilty again and a little more kindly toward her. Her life was obviously filled with hairy beasts and walking lunatics, and that could make anyone a little neurotic.

"Look, Fiona..." he said hesitantly as he put his hand on her shoulder.

She looked directly up into his face and he forgot what he meant to say. She stared at him, wide-eyed, breathing shallowly. She licked her lips. His gaze shifted to her mouth—pink, full, soft, inviting, enticing....

Before he knew it, he was leaning forward to kiss her, wanting with every fiber of his being to taste all that woman in such sweet and spicy form.

She let out her breath in a rush against his lips just before their mouths met. She jumped away from him as if he had leprosy. His eyes flashed up to meet hers. He saw surprise there for a split second before it was replaced by total outrage.

"Get out of my house this instant!"

"Let me ex—"

"I'm calling Morgan first thing in the morning to tell him I want someone else assigned to this case." Her voice was charged with fury. "And to think he called you his most capable associate! What kind of a place is he running there?"

"I might ask the same question about this place," Eli shot back. He held up his hand to ward off another angry retort. "Never mind. I'm too tired and sore to argue anymore tonight. Come hurl insults at me tomorrow morning. I'll be more responsive then."

"Where are you going?" she called as he stalked off into the night.

"Where else?" he flung over his shoulder. "Back to the kennel to look for clues and bandits and prowlers and murderers and muggers and fiends of every kind. Satisfied?"

Fiona figured he was probably too far away to hear the nasty word she uttered in his wake.

Four

Fiona confronted Eli at precisely nine-thirty the following morning. Her look could have frozen water. "Mr. Morgan is on the telephone," she said tersely. "He would like to speak to you."

Eli, who was talking with the locksmith they had rousted out of bed at the crack of dawn, hung his head for a moment, then went to the nearest telephone extension. He knew Fiona had spent the last ten minutes on the phone with Arthur. He glared at her with enough hostility to make her leave the room. If he was going to be chewed out by his boss, he damn well wasn't going to give her the satisfaction of listening.

"Hi, Art," he said into the receiver.

Arthur Morgan didn't yell. He didn't need to. With a combination of stern disapproval and guilt-inducing concern, he quickly had Eli apologizing for his behavior and promising to treat this job as seriously as if he were guarding the First Lady.

"The First Lady's dogs, you mean," Eli muttered.

Arthur continued extolling the importance of this case for another five minutes. Eli rolled his eyes, fidgeted like a teenaged kid, and punched the wall with his left hand. But he promised to do his best work and stay until the case was solved.

He hung up the phone and stared at it for a moment in tense silence. Then he cursed Arthur Morgan for reminding him so much of his father, he cursed Fiona for dragging him into this mess and he cursed himself for giving her good reason to call his employer with complaints.

When he had exhausted his considerable repertoire of unprintable phrases, he turned away from the phone. He stopped dead in his tracks. Two teenaged girls were staring at him with wide-eyed fascination.

Eli swallowed. "Uh, sorry girls. I, um . . ."

He heard a gleeful cackle from the doorway and glanced that way. Brian's mother, Ginny, was leaning against the doorjamb. "Don't worry about it, Eli. Around here, you're practically an amateur. Just don't let Fiona hear you talk like that. She was educated in a convent."

Eli forgot his consternation. "Really?"

Before he had time to pursue the subject, the air was rent by a blood-chilling shriek of horror. The sound came from the lobby. Acting on instinct, Eli shoved the three women into the feed room, shut the door, and ran toward the source of fearful cries, now coming from several people.

When he reached the hallway, Brian dashed past him at full speed. "Run for your life, man! It's Myron!" he screamed.

"Who's Myron?" Eli called after the boy's disappearing figure.

Instinct warned him he was in danger even before he heard a deep, guttural whoofing directly behind him. He whirled just in time to see an enormous furry monster fly through the air, baring two dozen sharp teeth as it leaped for his throat and knocked him to the ground.

Eli fell flat on his back. He nearly passed out when some two-hundred-fifty pounds of voracious canine landed on his chest. He raised his arms in a desperate attempt to shield his face and neck from the beast.

And he was *slobbered* on.

"What the—?" He snapped his mouth shut when the Saint Bernard's big pink tongue washed his face.

"Myron!" It was Fiona's voice, terse and exasperated. "Sit! Sit! Do you hear me? *Sit!*"

"No!" Eli cried. Too late. Myron sat.

"Oh, dear...." Fiona said, realizing her mistake. "Are you all right, Eli?"

"Get...him...off...me," Eli said through clenched teeth.

"Whoof!" said Myron. He pawed Eli in an attempt to make him stop playing dead, and his enormous claws left welts on Eli's face.

Fiona enlisted the help of Myron's apologetic owner. They each grabbed one side of the dog's collar. "He's gained weight, hasn't he?" Fiona said breathlessly. "Now one, two, three—yank!"

They pulled Myron off Eli. Fiona ordered the owner and three of her kennel girls to escort him back to his dog run. "And find that coward Brian and make him help you," she added. She turned back to Eli, who still lay prostrate on the floor with his eyes tightly closed. "Are you all right?"

"I think that monster just ruined my hopes of ever becoming a father," he said in a strained voice.

"Now, now, you're dramatizing," Fiona chided. "Get up."

"No," he said.

"Okay, but I feel obliged to warn you that you're lying right in the path between the lobby and the kennel wings. And I see a Shar-Pei at the front door right now."

Eli took her proffered hand and painfully hauled himself to his feet.

"Did you hit your head?" she asked.

"Yes," he muttered.

"Hurt your hand?"

"Yes."

"Twist your ankle?"

"Yes."

"Gosh, I'm sorry," she said with a noticeable lack of sincerity.

He scowled at her. Fiona smiled sweetly and walked away from him. He watched her cute little bottom in those tight, faded blue jeans until she was out of sight. Then he rubbed his aching head and spent a moment feeling sorry for himself.

It was less than an hour later that Fiona found the evidence. She immediately sent one of her teenaged staff—Eli's adoring fan club—to find him. When he appeared in the office, she showed him her computer screen.

"Someone tried to break into the system last night," she said.

He sat down at the machine with a slight frown on his face. "How do you know?"

"I just started to open this particular program," she explained. "I was the last person to use it. That was yesterday evening at about seven o'clock. But look at when the program was last activated."

Eli's frown deepened. "Just after midnight." Their eyes met. "When I was at your house and the kennel was deserted. I was so worried about you, I hightailed it out of here and left the door wide open. Anybody could have walked in." He slammed his hand against the desk. Then he winced—it had been his right hand.

"Somebody was here," she said with quiet force.

"Yes," he agreed, finally believing it. He ran his left hand over his scratched face. "What's on this program?"

"The list of all our current boarders. But I doubt if he actually saw that. You need the code word to break in. And no one knows the code word except me and Vicky. I'm sure about that. She arranged it that way to avoid billing errors."

Eli leaned back, thinking hard. "But why would anyone want a list of pets that are staying here?"

"I don't know." She looked down at him and instantly forgot her next comment. Instead she said, "Those scratches on your face look bad. Let me put something on them."

"No, it's all right," he said, waving away her concern.

"No, really."

"Fiona, I think this is more important at the moment."

She scowled stubbornly and began reciting a litany of all the terrible, fearsome germs he might get from dog scratches. "And since you're already carrying germs from that nasty bite on your hand . . . Are you all right? You suddenly look a little green," she said in alarm.

"I'll let you put anything you want on my scratches if you'll just stop talking about all these . . . disgusting parasites running around in my bloodstream," he said weakly.

"I wouldn't have thought a man in your line of work would be so squeamish," she chided.

She took his hand and led him back to the medicine cabinet in the kitchen. Everyone was hosing outsides, whatever *that* meant, so he had Fiona all to himself.

Her slim, graceful fingers opened and closed various cupboards until she found what she was looking for. He watched while she uncapped a bottle of hydrogen peroxide. He noticed her nails were long and shiny, and he realized she tried to take care of her hands despite her rough profession. She dabbed some of the liquid onto a cotton ball and peered up into his face. She stood on tiptoe.

Eli gave Fiona a heart-stopping grin. Really, he wasn't so bad when he wasn't acting superior, she decided charitably. Then she gasped when his hands slid around her waist and he effortlessly lifted her until she was sitting on the kitchen counter.

It made their heights almost level. It brought their eyes very close. His mouth was just inches from hers. His hands were warm on her waist, even through three layers of clothing. He squeezed her experimentally.

"You're so small," he murmured.

"But wiry." Her voice felt as if it was stuck in her throat.

"No." He rubbed his hand along her rib cage. "Wiry isn't the first word that comes to mind."

His hand was just inches below her breast. Even wearing this many clothes, that was a tantalizing thought. Then Fiona heard Ginny's voice on the intercom, and she let her breath out in a rush. Before she could hesitate again, she lifted her hand purposefully and dabbed hydrogen peroxide on Eli's face.

He winced.

"It shouldn't hurt," she said.

He grabbed her wrist. "It's not that. Why are you rubbing it in like you're trying to *erase* the scratches?"

"Oh. Sorry."

"Nervous?"

"No," she said nervously. She splashed some liquid onto a fresh cotton ball and decided to change the subject. "So now you finally believe someone is wandering around here at night?"

"Yes. Can you think of any reason an intruder would look through your files rather than steal cash or valuable equipment?"

"No. Wow, Myron got you good, didn't he?"

"This is proving to be my most dangerous case," Eli assured her.

She looked so earnest, dabbing at his wounds, Eli was tempted to provoke a little more sympathy in those wide blue-green eyes. If he had felt guilty before about not taking her seriously, he felt criminally negligent now that he was starting to believe her story. It made him want to be nice to her. Just because it was the right thing to do. Not because she smelled of scented soap and woman, or because her hair gleamed like silk under the lights, or even because her lushly rounded breasts would touch his chest if she leaned just a little farther forward.

"Do you have pets of wealthy people staying here?" he asked softly.

"Yes. Important people, too. State department officials, congressmen, senators, embassy personnel. There, you're done," she said breathlessly. She wrapped up her supplies and tossed her garbage into the plastic bin near Eli's feet.

She expected he would move away from her, but he didn't. He remained standing directly in front of her, his hands resting on the countertop on either side of her thighs.

"This leads to all sorts of interesting possibilities," he murmured.

"It does?" She blinked nervously.

Eli frowned thoughtfully and edged nearer to her, leaning one hip against the counter and shifting so his hard shoulder almost touched her breast. Fiona tried to scoot a little to one side and found her rib cage suddenly pressing against his arm. She drew a sharp breath. The sneaky devil had moved his hands closer to her thighs without her noticing. She didn't understand how his right arm could look so sexy with all those bandages wrapped around it.

"It could mean something important," Eli whispered.

The golden brown softness of his gaze traveled consideringly over her face and hair. Fiona's gaze dropped shyly to the open neck of his flannel shirt. His stance drew the material away from the smooth, heavy column of his throat. She could see that his skin was firm and golden with good health, smooth and hard like the marble statue of a god. But Eli wasn't cold and inert like marble. His body heat was engulfing her, warming her with delicious little sparks of excitement, and the force of his sensuality was making her lips part involuntarily and her breasts fill with heavy longing.

"What...means something important?" she croaked, hypnotized by his probing eyes. His lashes drooped over his eyes. His lips parted slightly. Fiona's chest started to rise and fall rapidly as she gulped in excited little breaths.

"Fiona?" he asked softly, hesitating.

She slid her hand up his arm in answer, delightedly rubbing the smoothly molded muscles barely concealed by his layers of clothing. "Yes," she said with certainty. She wanted this. She had wanted to feel his kiss since the first moment she saw him.

He didn't hesitate again but slid his hands around her back and drew her toward him with easy strength, almost lifting her off the counter as he fitted their bodies together, chest to chest, belly to belly, and their hips... Fiona gave a tiny groan as he nestled into the inviting juncture of her thighs.

"Mmm." He sighed and nuzzled his way along her cheek until he found her mouth with his.

The first touch of his lips against hers was a shock, sweeter than she had imagined, more powerful than she had allowed herself to fantasize. Fiona wanted to devour him instantly, starving for him, for his affection, for his strong arms and warm, protective body against hers. She grasped his arms tightly and willed herself to let him set the pace, to just enjoy him while she could.

And he *was* enjoyable. There was no doubt that he knew exactly what he was doing. His lips rubbed and caressed hers with a heady combination of insistence and delicacy, taking and giving pleasure, exploring and teasing. When the swirling blackness behind her eyes became too overwhelming, Fiona opened them slightly. Eli's eyes were still closed, and the intense absorption on his face as he kissed her made her insides contract with painful desire.

Eli pulled back. "Fiona, Fiona," he whispered between harsh breaths of air. He opened his eyes, and the hot golden glitter she saw there made her press herself closer to him.

Their mouths sought each other again, slanting across one another with open hunger this time. Fiona gave herself up to the swirling blackness now, assured that he felt it, too. She felt his tongue, hot and silky and agile, probing the full shape of her lower lip, felt his sure, confident hands pull her shirt out of her jeans and slip underneath—

"Fi-ona! How could you?"

Eli and Fiona broke apart like guilty teenagers and both turned their heads just in time to see Brian stomp into the kitchen. Dressed in the most elaborate winter gear Eli had ever seen, from his thigh-high rubber boots to his furry Tibetan-style hat, the boy came to a sudden halt as he stared at the two of them still melded together with their arms wrapped around each other.

"*Ohhhh.* Oh-ho! Ah-hah!" Brian's face contorted somewhere between a smirk and a leer. "Well, well, well."

Fiona loosened the death grip her knees had on Eli's hips and slid backward on the countertop into a slightly less compromising position.

"Gee, guys, I'm sorry if I interrupted anything," Brian cooed.

"You didn't," Fiona said crossly. "I was just trying to revive him after what *you* let Myron do to him."

Impervious to insult, Brian confided to Eli, "Fifi is such a samaritan."

Eli wisely decided to maintain a diplomatic silence. He leaned against the counter again and tried to look casual. He was uncomfortably aware that if he had been left alone with Fiona for just a minute longer, looking casual would have been physically impossible.

How could he have been so stupid? They were necking like teenage kids right in the line of traffic. With almost the full staff of twenty on duty today, it was only surprising that he had found even a moment alone with Fiona. He glanced at her and saw that her face was pink with embarrassment as she rearranged her clothes under Brian's interested stare.

Personally, Eli was thankful the kid had interrupted them when he did. Another minute, and he would have been pulling up Fiona's long underwear so he could touch her full breasts with their hard, delicate little nipples, kiss the silken skin of her smooth belly, investigate the promising heat between her—

That's enough, he warned himself. He hopped onto the counter next to Fiona, hoping a sitting position would help camouflage his condition until he calmed down and started acting like an adult. He met her flustered expression and grinned. She was so adorable.

"Standing there, staring at me will not get the work done any faster," she informed Brian.

"Hey, man, that's what I want to talk to you about. Like, how can you be so unfair? What have I ever done to you? How can you *do* this to me?" Brian stomped up and down the length of the kitchen, waving his arms to emphasize his outrage.

Fiona rolled her eyes. "What's wrong?"

"You put Myron *and* Rocky Snyder in my wing!" he said accusingly. "I could handle one without complaint—"

"I seriously doubt that."

"But *both* of them! It's just too much. It smacks of persecution. You think you can bully me because I'm the only guy here."

"I'm here," Eli reminded him.

"Yeah, and you're the walking wounded. Two days on the premises, and look at you. If you keep this up, we're going to have to get a wheelchair for you soon," Brian said rudely.

"All right, Brian," Fiona interjected tiredly. "I'm sorry I stuck you with Myron and Rocky, but it's done now, and you might as well make the best of it."

Seeing another storm on the horizon, Eli foolishly tried to intercede. "Isn't Rocky the dog that the karate teacher and the judo teacher are fighting a custody battle over? How's he doing?"

Brian's whole face screwed up. "Disgusting! He's dirty and he's messy and he stinks. It took me ten minutes to hose his run clean today." He closed his eyes and managed to look pale for a moment. "I don't think I can go through something like that again, Fiona."

"I'll see what I can do, Brian," Fiona said, giving in. She just wanted to end the whole embarrassing scene. "Now get back to work," she ordered in her best bosslike voice.

Seeing that Brian intended to continue stalling, Eli said, "Do what she says, kid. She's too busy to fool around today."

"Straight from the horse's mouth," Brian said cockily and sailed out the door. Fiona rolled her eyes while Eli laughed.

"I kind of like him," Eli admitted ruefully.

"You'll outgrow it."

Eli smiled at her and smoothed her hair away from her face. Her lips were still pink and slightly swollen from his kisses. "Uh, Fiona, did you—I mean, are we..." He cleared his throat, preparatory to trying again.

"Yo! Mr. Becker! Can you come here for a second?"

Eli's head dropped forward in defeat when he heard the locksmith's voice calling to him from the next room. "I'll be right there," he called. He gave Fiona a fierce look. "We're going to talk about this later," he warned her.

Fiona sat alone on the counter for a moment with her hands folded and her feet swinging like a little kid's. And what, she wondered, would they both say?

She hopped off the counter as soon as she heard her name called over the intercom. She spent the next two hours snowed under by the demands of over twenty customers who checked in during that time, as well as organizing and galvanizing her staff, storing supplies which arrived at the last minute and begging the furnace-repair man to come out and determine why the furnace was making funny noises.

Eli searched for Fiona that afternoon, intending to tell her that all the locks were finally changed. He wanted to know exactly to whom she intended to distribute keys.

He finally found her in the office, standing by the window with the telephone receiver pressed against her ear. Her chestnut curls gleamed darkly in the afternoon sunlight. Her bulky clothing hinted erotically at all the slim lines and lush curves that lay hidden beneath them. Eli stopped in his tracks when Fiona turned wide, disturbed eyes toward him and shook her head in distress.

"Oh, no," she groaned.

Eli wondered what the customer on the other end of the line was saying to upset her so.

"I can't handle this," she muttered. She shook her head one more time and then slammed the telephone down. She looked forlornly out the window and said, "Oh, God, please don't do this to me."

Eli came forward and took her hands in his. They felt small and fragile. "What's wrong?"

She lowered her head, but not before he had seen her face contort with pain. It twisted his heart. He wanted to protect her.

"Fiona? What did he say?" he asked gently.

"Eighty per cent chance of snow. Accumulation of five to seven inches by Christmas Day."

He stared blankly. "What?"

"Winds from the northwest gusting up to eighteen miles per hour."

"Fiona—"

"Temperatures dropping into the low teens tonight. The cold spell will last until after Christmas," she continued morosely, pouring her heart out.

"You were listening to the weatherman?" he snapped, feeling ridiculous.

She nodded. "I call him five or six times a day." She pulled her hands out of his and plopped dispiritedly into a chair. "This Christmas is sure turning out to be my baptism by fire."

"Fiona..." he began.

"Brace yourselves!" cried Ginny, dashing into the office with two girls in hot pursuit. "They're piling up out there." Ginny and the girls started arming themselves with leashes and towels.

Within seconds the door to the lobby burst open and customer after customer piled in, leading or being led by an assortment of boisterous pets. Eli glanced at Fiona in astonishment.

"It's called a rush," she explained, slightly amused by the way he lunged out of the line of fire and pressed himself against the wall as more of her staff scurried past him.

Within moments the entire front of the kennel was full of barking dogs, yowling cats, bickering people, a rabbit, a gerbil and two turtles.

"What? No partridge?" said Eli.

Naturally the phone started ringing off the hook. Fiona was running back and forth, waiting on customers, answering the phone and doling out instructions to her staff. Eli hung around, hoping the uproar would die down long enough for him to talk to her about the new locks and keys. He also had every intention of talking to her about more personal matters, but he was fast learning to wait until after business hours.

When a three-dog fight started in the lobby, Fiona flew into the middle of the fray. Eli followed hot on her heels, certain she was going to get herself killed. Brian showed some mettle by picking up the biggest of the three and dragging him into a corner. Fiona snatched up the littlest one and shoved him into Eli's arms.

Before anyone could move another step, a customer screamed, "What the hell is *that*?"

They all turned to see Nadine leading a freshly groomed Old English sheepdog into the lobby. "It's your dog," she told the man.

"That's not *my* dog!"

Fiona assured him it was.

"What have you *done* to it?" he cried, his diamond pinkie ring flashing light as he waved his arms around hysterically.

Everyone looked at Fiona. The customers had all gone silent, riveted with fascination. Fiona regarded the skinny dog, who now only had about a quarter inch of hair all over, where once he had resembled a polar bear. Nadine had put bows on his ears in a sad attempt to distract from his virtual nudity.

Fiona sighed. "When you brought the dog in, sir, we explained that his hair was so matted he would have to be shaved down to the skin."

"I said to leave as much hair on him as you could!"

"I did," Nadine snapped, clearly losing her patience. "And if you took care of him and condescended to brush him once in a while, he wouldn't get in that disgusting condition!"

"You're just too lazy to brush him out!" the man accused.

"Nadine, I'll handle this," Fiona said tersely. She took the dog and shoved the woman toward the kitchen. "As I explained this morning, sir, not only would brushing out a dog in that condition take several days and cost you a few hundred dollars due to the valuable hours the groomer would have to spend with him—"

"You people are robbers!"

Fiona pursed her lips. "I also pointed out that brushing out such thick, heavy mats would put your dog through considerable and totally unnecessary pain."

"Unnecessary?" the man repeated incredulously. "Just look at this miserable beast! He looks like a drowned rat!"

Fiona could feel her normally equable temper begin to fray. "*He* doesn't care how he looks, and he would be the one to suffer for your vanity. If his long hair is so important to you, I suggest you follow Nadine's advice and take proper care of him."

The man started to curse Fiona with loud, viciously insulting phrases. Eli had heard all he intended to. Clutching his little captive Pekingese in his good arm, he stalked forward and said, "Miss Larkin has been more than patient with you, mister. I suggest you leave before you embarrass yourself any further."

"I demand a refund!"

"Get out of here now, or I'll throw you out," Eli warned steadily.

The man turned purple with rage. "I'll sue you people for every penny you've got! I'll turn your name to mud! I'll—"

"Be sorry if you don't shut up and leave," Eli interrupted.

The man jerked his dog's leash out of Fiona's hands, yanking so hard that the dog stumbled and whimpered. Overcome with a sense of helpless pity, Fiona tried to snatch the leash back. "Stop that! You're hurting him!"

"Get your hands off me!" the man snarled. "You're going to be sorry for this, young woman! If I ever catch you out of sight of your bodyguard here, I'll make you regret this." With that parting shot, he slammed the door so hard the Christmas decorations fell off it. A minute later he peeled his car out of the driveway, making sure to leave deep ruts on the lawn in front of the door.

"Good Lord," said Eli, following Fiona back into the office.

"The weirdos come out at Christmas," she admitted, taking the Pekingese from him. It barked and licked her face.

"I can't believe someone threatened you because he didn't like the way his dog was groomed," Eli said in amazement.

"It happens all the time. Especially with people like that who won't take care of their dogs themselves. And it really burns me up, too, because Nadine is such a great groomer."

"Really?"

"Yes, she—"

"No, I mean do people really blow their stack and threaten you all the time?"

"Oh. Yes. Not regular, year-round customers. But as you can tell, we get a lot of really bizarre people at this time of year."

"Did someone threaten you before your troubles started and you called Morgan's?"

She frowned thoughtfully, realizing what he was getting at. "Yes. Several people have threatened us since the beginning of the season. Even since the beginning of the year. And this is the first time I've ever been here alone at night, without Vicky and Race."

Eli sat down and stretched his legs out. "We have too much motive and too little crime," he muttered.

"What do you mean?"

"You have VIP dogs staying here, which indicates all sorts of twisted possibilities for extortion, ransom, dognapping and espionage. You get threatened with lawsuits and violence, which makes me expect vandalism and physical assault. You keep valuable equipment and some money on the property, but there's been no robbery.

"There are a dozen reasons someone could be trying to break in here, yet none of them fit the scenario. If you're right, someone has come here four times at night and done nothing, taken nothing, seen nothing important. So far, trespassing seems to be the only offense in this case. I don't get it."

"You still think it's just an employee or ex-employee letting herself in for obscure but harmless reasons?"

He shrugged. "At the moment, I still think it's harmless," he admitted. "And I also think that changing the locks was the most logical step in ending these midnight visits." But the desire to protect her was growing stronger inside him, and he wouldn't close the case until he was certain she was in no danger.

"I need to talk to you about the keys," he added, forcing himself to sublimate his personal feelings for the moment.

"Okay. Let me just give this dog to one of the kids." She pulled her hair out of the Pekingese's mouth and called a new kid named Christina into the office.

Christina entered the room looking filthy. She was covered with water, mud, canned dog food, hair, dust and other substances that Eli didn't even want to speculate on. Her young face looked petulant and resentful. When Fiona asked her to put the Pekingese in its run, the girl hurled her leash on the floor and started shouting at Fiona.

"I quit! I'm sick of this place! All I do is clean and feed, clean and feed!"

"But you—"

"Oh, sure! Once in a while I get to haul a thousand pounds of dog food into the feed room or help you store bottles of bleach and liquid soap. What kind of a place is this?"

"We have to—"

"I thought I'd get to play with dogs, not muck out their runs twenty times a day!"

Fiona sighed. Eli said, "Grow up, kid. No one pays you to play."

"That's not fair!"

Fiona wiped a hand across her tired face. "You could play with dogs while you're cleaning them, or on your breaks. Instead, Christina, you rush through your work as fast as you can so you can go sit in the staff room, smoke and watch TV," she said quietly. "Vicky told you when she hired you that it was hard, messy work."

The girl looked near to tears. "Well, I don't want to do it anymore. I quit!" She turned and ran from the room.

"Does that happen often?" Eli asked Fiona.

Fiona nodded wearily. "Vicky's a pretty good judge of potential, but at least one kid per season can't take the heat." She shrugged. "I know it's a tough job, but this place has a lot of rewards, too. Some people just can't appreciate that."

"Does this leave you shorthanded?"

"Yes." She smiled ruefully. "We're fast approaching that point at which things can't possibly get any worse."

It would be a long time before he realized what insane impulse seized him at that moment. "Look, Fiona, I'll be happy to help out as long as I'm here."

She stared at him in surprise. "You don't have to do that."

"I want to help you. Just show me what to do. I catch on fast."

"Are you sure you know what you're doing?"

He grinned. "I think temporary insanity has taken hold of me ever since I met you."

Five

That afternoon Eli learned what "hosing outsides" meant. It meant he put on as many warm clothes as he could find and went outside to wash down his fair share of the kennel's two hundred dog runs with high-pressure hoses. Fiona insisted they be spotless when the staff was done. After finishing, Eli wrapped a blanket around his sodden body and miserably sipped hot coffee while Brian cheerfully initiated him into the glamorous world of the kennel worker.

"This isn't so bad. We only hose outsides four times a day in winter. In summer, we do it once every hour from seven in the morning until ten at night."

"I don't want to hear this," Eli said morosely.

"Now, of course, if we get hit by this blizzard Fiona's worried about, things could get grim," Brian continued.

"Things are *already* grim."

"Then we'll have to shovel all two hundred runs. And let me tell you, that's no picnic."

"*Hosing* them is no picnic."

Fiona dashed through the staff room. She stopped for a moment and scowled at both of them. "Why are you both sitting here doing nothing?" she demanded. "If you're bored you can do the laundry which is backed up, or sweep and mop the entire back hall which is a mess, or go scoop the front yard which is full of—"

"Don't tell me," Eli pleaded.

"There's afternoon feedings, afternoon medications, sani-cleaning, and food pans to be washed. I need a list of dogs that will need blankets tonight, and someone's got to go to the store and get me thirty bottles of bleach." Fiona folded her arms. "Well? What'll it be?"

Eli hauled himself stiffly to his feet. "I'll go do the laundry, since it sounds like I can at least stay warm and dry doing that. In the meantime," he added, wanting to remind her why he was really here, "I need a record of everyone who's threatened you, Vicky, or Oak Hill recently. I also want to see the files of all VIP dogs that have been here since the night of the first disturbance."

Fiona nodded and left the room. Behind her, she heard Eli mutter, "No wonder that girl quit. Who would put up with this kind of torture?"

By closing time, she felt fairly sorry for him. He was doing his best to help out, and a hotshot international security consultant probably wasn't used to slogging around all day in a messy, tiring job where the boarders couldn't say "thank you" and the customers apparently didn't know how to.

Since it was still hours before midnight, the hour during which the previous disturbances had occurred, Fiona offered Eli a nap in her cottage. "You won't get much sleep here in the kennel while the kids are still working," she explained.

He agreed with that assessment, since she had to shout to make herself heard above the uproar. He followed her home through the dark oak grove, admiring her beautifully shaped bottom as she flashed in and out of the moonlit trail ahead of him. He admitted to himself that he had craned his neck to watch the subtle sway of her hips every time she had walked by him all day.

The smooth firmness of her thighs hugged by the faded denim of her blue jeans enthralled him. The way they extended alluringly from beneath the hem of her baggy, oversize sweater struck him as the sexiest thing he'd ever seen. And the slender fragility of her wrists, dwarfed by her rolled-up woolen cuffs, made him long to press his lips to the soft scented skin where her pulse beat, warm and vibrant.

Why was it that when everyone else, himself included, looked like hell by the end of a full day's work at the kennel, Fiona still looked so pretty and smelled so good? Her hair was a little messy now, but it still shone with healthy highlights and smelled as sweet as her ivory skin. Her face was drawn and tired, but her clear aqua eyes still sparkled, highlighted by the faint pink glow on her cheeks.

Oh, Fiona. He remembered the honeyed taste of her mouth, the way she sank against him and gripped him between her legs, the way those small hands had touched and stroked him....

Eli swallowed hard. They were nearly at her cottage. She looked back at him and smiled faintly, her lovely expression caught by the dim lights from her windows. He was going to be alone with her for the next few hours, alone in a warm, dry, quiet house, and nothing was going to stop them from—

"Tidbit!" Fiona exclaimed. "What have you been doing?"

"What?" said Eli. He heard the excited catch in his own voice and realized his fantasies were getting out of control again.

Fiona stooped to pick up a dog the size of a small rabbit.

The sound of Fiona's voice unleashed a torrent of happy, noisy greetings a moment later. The barking and mewling made Eli blink. He liked to think that a lesser man would have cringed in horror. Within moments, all of Fiona's dogs and cats came running around from the back of the house to greet her and Eli with muddy paws, drooling muzzles, high-pitched whines, manly little barks, and petulant meows.

"Oh, my God," Eli said. He had forgotten about her pets. How could he have forgotten that she shared her four-room cottage with enough animals to fill a small zoo? His wonderful erotic fantasies shriveled to dust in the cold glare of furry reality.

"You're all so muddy!" Fiona said. She scowled. "You've been chasing the ducks again, haven't you?" The biggest dog wagged its tail and tried to look innocent, despite the layers of mud clinging to its long black hair. Fiona looked at it despairingly and said, "Oh, Sylvester, I'll have to give you a bath."

"Sylvester?" Eli asked, dodging the dog's wagging tail.

"After Stallone. There's a certain resemblance, don't you think?" She looked at him apologetically. "I'm going to have to clean them all off and feed them. Why don't you go inside and wash up?"

"No, no," he said, feeling like a martyr. "I'll help you."

She insisted it wasn't necessary, and he insisted he couldn't just sit relaxing inside her house while she tackled the dirty dozen alone outside. It took them nearly an hour to towel off all the dogs while the cats sat around and watched with fastidious distaste. Then the monsters all had to be fed. By the time Eli followed Fiona inside the house, he felt he had never been so exhausted in his life.

"Sit down. I'll make something to eat," she told him. She washed her hands and face and started moving around the small kitchen with easy familiarity. The rest of her was still pretty muddy, and her fatigue was evident in her whole body, but everything about her still entranced Eli. It was a shame he was too damn tired to do anything about it. Anyhow, as soon as her pets were all done eating, they'd probably come piling through the dog flap installed near the kitchen and interrupt anything he wanted to do with Fiona. Eli gave a deep sigh and buried his face in his arms which rested on the kitchen table.

Fiona smiled at Eli's dramatic posture. It reminded her of Brian, and she suddenly wondered how much Eli had been like that exasperating young man fifteen years ago. "You've had a hard day, haven't you?"

He groaned feelingly and nodded without raising his head.

"I guess this isn't the sort of job you envisioned when you started working for Mr. Morgan."

"This isn't the sort of job I've envisioned in my worst nightmares."

She laughed at that and put some hamburgers under the broiler. She knew without asking that he would be very hungry after today's hard work. "I really appreciate your offering to pitch in, especially with your sore hand. And you must be aching a little from your first meeting with Myron, too."

"That dog is a menace to society." Eli raised his head just enough to prop it lazily on his left fist. He regarded her with weary amusement. "Why don't they train that beast?"

"They've tried. There's an obedience instructor who works here spring, summer and autumn, when it's warm enough to teach classes outside. He's even given private crash courses to Myron. Nothing works. Myron just can't understand why a two-hundred-fifty-pound Saint Bernard shouldn't act like a frisky twelve-pound poodle."

"At least he's friendly. Do you ever get mean dogs his size?"

"Sometimes. Do you want corn or green beans?"

"Both. This is nice of you, Fiona. You don't have to cook me dinner, you know."

She shrugged. "You didn't have to lend a hand today. Anyhow," she admitted, "you and I haven't gotten off to the best start, and I'm trying to be civil."

"I'm trying, too."

"I've noticed," she said dryly.

"It doesn't always work out," he admitted sheepishly. "Patience isn't really my strong point."

She smiled. "Kennel work takes a lot of patience."

He looked at her curiously. "You really love it here, don't you?"

"Is that so surprising?"

"Well, it's hard, messy work. And a lot of responsibility. I saw that woman who burst into tears today and begged you to take good care of her dog because she loves it more than she loves her husband and kids." He shook his head in amazement. "You're affected by weather conditions. You have staff problems. Your clients are *all* crazy, even the nice ones. At the moment, it's a little hard to figure out why you love it."

She started toasting some hamburger buns. "I like the responsibility. It makes me feel useful and important. I don't mind crazy clients if they're nice. You have staff problems in any business." She tilted her head and thought about it for a moment. "I guess I love it because it's so varied. I work with people and animals, and I like both. I have to know about all sorts of things—first aid, supply and demand, management, financial matters, plumbing, electricity, advertising, public relations. It's always interesting."

"Well, I have to admit that there hasn't been a dull moment so far," he said wryly.

"Anyhow, I have a real home here. The permanent staff are like my family, all the customers know me and I have someplace to keep all my pets."

"That's important," he agreed, warily eyeing a few dogs who barreled through the dog flap and made their way into the living room.

"How do you like your burgers?"

"Medium-rare. You said you've been here since June. What did you do before that?"

"I was in hotel management."

"So what made you switch to pet motel management?" he asked curiously.

"After I acquired my second dog and third cat, the hotel I was living in decided things had gone too far. They told me to get rid of my animals or leave."

"So you left?"

She nodded. "Getting rid of a living thing, like it was just so much extra baggage, was out of the question. In fact, that was how I acquired them. Some filthy...slime had dumped them in each case, leaving them to starve and fend for themselves. It just infuriates me." She slapped a plate down in front of him.

"So I stalled the hotel and tried to find a job where I could keep my animals. I was interviewing at a country inn not far from here when I read in the local paper that Oak Hill Pet Motel was looking for a live-in assistant manager. I called Vicky and then drove right over for the interview."

"Was there a lot of competition?"

She shrugged. "Some, but Vicky and I both realized right away that I was perfect for the job. I already knew something about running a service business like this, I had good recommendations, I knew a lot about dogs through necessity and I desperately needed a place to live. What's more, Vicky and I hit it off right away," she added. "That's important, because she's not exactly the easiest person in the world to get along with. And we complement each other well in business, too. I'm pretty good with people—staff, customers, workmen. And Vicky has an amazing flair with animals. There are only two dogs I've ever seen that she couldn't make friends with, and I'm convinced they were both psychopaths."

The mention of dogs made Eli think of another question. "You said you had two dogs and three cats when you started to work here?"

"That's right. Do you want cheeseburgers?"

"Yes, please. Does that mean you've acquired all these other animals since you came here?"

"Uh-huh."

"In just seven months?" he asked incredulously. No wonder Brian said things were getting out of hand.

"Do you want ketchup?"

"Fiona! How can you have acquired—" he paused for a minute to count "four dogs, four cats and a bird in such a short time?"

She put his cheeseburgers on his plate. "They were abandoned. Some people drop their pets off here with no intention of ever coming back for them."

Eli looked at her in surprise as she finished putting the rest of the food on the table. "But don't you guys take down lots of data about the owners? Names, addresses, emergency numbers?"

She sat down opposite him. "Yes. But we don't demand verification or anything. Some people lie, some move and some tell the truth but just never respond to our demands that they come back for their pet." She put her napkin on her lap and said, "Dig in."

He was hungry enough to be distracted for a moment. Halfway through his first burger he slowed down and pursued the subject again. "Can't you call the authorities about something like that?"

"You can," she admitted, "but it doesn't usually have much effect. Crimes against animals are pretty low on their list of priorities. In fact, the only real legal weight we've ever managed to bring against anyone is for nonpayment rather than abandonment."

"You mean like the guy that Brian mentioned last night? The one who stiffed you?"

"The one the Morgan agency let slip away."

"That had nothing to do with me," he reminded her. "I was still in the navy in those days."

"You were in the navy?" she asked in astonishment.

"Is that so surprising?" he countered.

"Well . . . You just don't seem very military to me."

"How so? Hey, you make a pretty good burger."

"Thanks. I mean, your hair is long and your clothes are casual, you hate getting up early, you seem, uh, a little resistant to order and authority, you're cranky—"

"I am not!"

"Let's say you express yourself very freely," she amended.

"Yeah, well, those are some of the reasons I decided to drop out in the end."

"Were you an officer?"

"Yeah. I went to the academy in Annapolis. The whole bit."

"What was your job?"

"I was in Naval Intelligence."

"Really?" Her eyes were as wide as the summer sky, and just as bright. "That sounds exciting."

"It had its moments."

"Can you tell me about it?"

She looked so awed, he couldn't resist the temptation. He looked at her mysteriously and said, "I could, but then I'd have to kill you."

Her gasp make him laugh. A moment later she scowled at him. "You're teasing me."

"Well, I guess I wouldn't really terminate you. But we'd probably both get arrested, anyhow."

"So your work was top secret? Confidential? For your eyes only?"

He grinned. "You've seen too many movies. Actually, most of it would probably bore you silly. Security stuff."

"Like this job?"

"Nothing like this job. Nothing in my life has been remotely like this job." *And no one has been remotely like you.*

"So how'd you wind up with Mr. Morgan?"

"I knew him in the service. He was a great commanding officer and a good friend. When I started showing signs of cabin fever, he started urging me to resign my commission and go to work for him."

"He must have a lot of confidence in you," she mused.

"He does." He reached across the table and took her hand. "I wish you could, too, Fiona. I know we've had our differences, and I know I began this job with a bad attitude, but I promise you I won't let anything happen to you or Oak Hill."

Fiona stared at him in silence. His hand was hard and reassuring, and the way his fingers felt as they stroked her palm made her insides quiver with longing. His eyes were dark and soft as he gazed at her earnestly. She could tell by his expression that her feelings of mingled doubt and desire were written all over her face. After a long, quiet moment, he released her hand and concentrated on his dinner again.

Fiona poked at her vegetables for a while. Finally, in an effort to break the silence, she said, "I've never even asked you if you like dogs."

"I like them fine. I just feel a little overwhelmed by them at the moment." He smiled at her. "You must work like a... I mean, you must work hard to keep this house so clean with thirteen pets."

"Fourteen. Don't forget my bird, Mrs. Periwinkle."

"A bird was abandoned here, too?"

Fiona nodded. "She's the meanest lovebird in the world. When her owners got divorced, neither one of them would take her. She wound up living at the kennel until the staff rebelled."

"Why did the staff rebel over a bird?"

Fiona grimaced. "You wouldn't ask that if you have ever tried to clean her cage."

"So why did you take her?"

"Well, *someone* had to."

"Judging by the size of your menagerie, Fiona, you seem to be the 'someone' in every case. Vicky only has one dog. You have six."

She shrugged. "I feel very strongly about abandonment. If I didn't take them in, they'd wind up in dire straits, if they lived at all. Of course," she added pointedly, "if other people would adopt some of them, the burden wouldn't fall on me every time."

"I sense you're leading up to something," he said resignedly.

"I am. Finish your vegetables," she ordered.

"Yes, ma'am."

"There's a golden retriever staying at the kennel right now. He's six months old, and now that he's not a cute little puppy anymore, his owner doesn't want him. We...had words about it, but she's not coming back for him. She told me to find a home for him or he goes straight to the dog pound." She looked at him expectantly.

He sighed. "Fiona, I can scarcely remember the last time I slept. Every inch of my body aches. I'm still facing an all-night vigil at the kennel, and I have to plow through all those files you pulled for me about people who have threatened you guys. I have enough to think about right now." The disappointed look on her face made him feel like a bum.

"I thought... Oh, never mind what I thought," she said wearily. "Do you want anything else to eat?"

"No, thanks." He tried to think of a way to make amends. Then he felt angry at having to make amends for not offering to adopt a dog he had never seen and couldn't care for properly. She was a maddening woman! And he was a fool, sitting here getting friendly with the client. Not to mention fantasizing about the client, he thought with self-disgust. Better to stick to business, finish the job and get home to his family.

His family! He hadn't called them since breaking the bad news to them two days ago. He'd better phone them now to tell them this case was taking a little longer than he had anticipated.

"Do you mind if I use your phone for a collect call?" he asked hesitantly as Fiona cleared the table.

"No, go right ahead."

She was behaving irrationally, but she couldn't seem to help herself. She knew she had reached her limit, that her little house couldn't hold another animal. However, it wasn't Eli's responsibility to adopt a dog she couldn't bear to send to the pound.

The look in the golden retriever's eyes was too familiar to Fiona. She had seen it in other eyes. She had seen it in her own eyes every time she had looked in the mirror for many years.

But that was a long time ago, she reminded herself silently. And it was unreasonable to pressure Eli because someone else had abandoned another dog. It wasn't Eli's problem.

But she silently acknowledged that she wanted Eli to be different from other people. She was drawn to him, and she wanted to believe she could never be drawn to someone who could be insensitive to an abandoned dog. Or child. . . .

The thought came to her unbidden that she wanted Eli to be the sort of man who took in strays.

"Hi, Mom," he said into the phone.

Fiona stiffened when she realized he was calling his family. The family he wanted to spend Christmas with. Fiona rolled her eyes. How could she have forgotten for even five minutes that it was Christmas? The reason to be jolly, the time for families to come together. *Ho, ho, ho.* She scrubbed the broiler pan furiously.

She tried not to listen to his conversation with his mother, his father, his brother, his sister, his niece, his nephew... Good Lord, just how big was his family? She *tried* not to listen, but the affection and fondness in his voice shivered through her and made her envious. Envious of him for having them, but mostly envious of them for having him.

Stop it, stop it. This season always had a bad effect on her. She knew it, she should be prepared for it by now and not lose her head. But when she heard him promise his mother he would do his best to be home for Christmas, just three days away, it took an enormous effort of will for her to keep her face impassive.

Of course he would leave. She had never thought otherwise. He would go back to his life, and she would stay here alone. Nothing else had ever occurred to her.

Nevertheless, the moment Eli hung up the phone, Fiona asked in an icy voice, "So you think you'll have it wrapped up by Christmas Eve?"

"Yes," he said briefly. "Want help with the dishes?"

"No." She felt his gaze on her back.

"Fiona," he began hesitantly.

"What?"

"If nothing else happens between now and Christmas Eve, there's no reason I can't go home for at least a couple of days."

Her lips tightened. She concentrated on her scrubbing and said as evenly as possible, "Even if nothing else happens, we don't know why someone has been trespassing, or what his intentions are, or if he'll return when you leave."

"Look, if that's what's worrying you..." His voice trailed off. Fiona gasped when she felt two strong hands grab her from behind and turn her around to face him. "Look at me when we're talking, would you?" he snapped.

"All right," she said stonily.

Eli made an obvious effort to regain his patience. "If you're worried that your trespasser will come back after I leave, I'll get one of the kids from the agency to spend a few nights in the kennel while I'm in Wisconsin.''

"Kids?"

"Yeah. Junior staff. They're young and fairly inexperienced, but they're all certainly qualified to handle a stakeout."

"I might as well forget the agency and just pay Brian to sleep in the kennel, in that case," she said acidly.

Eli counted to ten while Fiona dried her hands. He followed her into the living room a moment later. "Will you at least make some meager attempt to be reasonable?"

"Twenty minutes ago you said you wouldn't let anything happen to me or Oak Hill. Now you're planning to leave by Christmas Eve no matter what. And *I'm* unreasonable?"

"I told you all along I wanted to be with my family for Christmas! I told you that this will be the first time we've all been together in ten years. I told you how my parents are counting on me to get home in time for it. For God's sake, Fiona, wouldn't you try not to disappoint them if you were me?"

That brought her to a dead halt. She picked up Tidbit and stroked her, trying to cover her sudden discomfort and embarrassment. This rotten holiday meant such a lot to Eli. And while it was true that someone was playing games with them at Oak Hill, the intruder didn't seem to intend any physical violence or theft.

Fiona took a deep breath and tried to be conciliatory. "I'm sorry, Eli. I guess to someone who's worked in Naval Intelligence, someone who protects people from terrorism, espionage and death threats, what's going on here must seem pretty unimportant."

"I didn't mean—"

"But nothing like this has ever happened here before, so it seems very serious to me."

"Fiona . . ."

"I will try to trust your professional judgment and be more reasonable."

He felt like a heel again. She looked so tense, as if she was holding herself together through sheer willpower. In sudden, tender concern, he said, "You must be exhausted."

Her eyes gratefully acknowledged the unspoken truce he had just offered her. "You must be pretty beat, too." She made a little sound and put Tidbit back down. "I invited you here to take a nap before you go on duty tonight, and now I've wasted nearly two hours."

"That's okay. You fed me," he said softly.

"And you helped feed my dogs," she countered. "Come into the bedroom. You can still get a few hours' sleep before you have to leave."

Eli's stomach contracted as she took his hand and led him into her bedroom without the slightest hesitation. It was small and rustic, like the rest of the house, with a brass double bed covered by a thick comforter. Feminine and sturdy, like Fiona.

He pictured her lying in that bed with her dark curls spread across the pillow and her pale skin flushed with sleep, rosy and soft against the white sheets. He started breathing a little faster.

"Maybe I should just lie down on the couch," he said in a strained voice.

"No, my dogs would think you want to play. If you're in here, I can shut the door and you can have some peace and quiet."

He didn't think he would get any peace sleeping on pillows that bore her fragrant scent, but he didn't know how to say so without saying a lot of other things to her, too. So he said, "Okay."

"Here." She picked up a quilt from the wooden chair by her dresser. It was soft and worn. "You can even use my favorite quilt." She touched his arm and frowned. "Eli, you're soaked!"

"It took me a while to get the hang of hosing the dog runs without hosing myself," he admitted wryly.

"You should have said something. You shouldn't sit around in wet clothes in this cold weather." She clucked over him with motherly concern, and he laughed at how cute it made her look.

She tried to insist he take off his clothes so she could wash and dry them while he slept. He protested vehemently, his whole body trembling at the thought of sleeping naked in her bed. When her face took on that stubborn expression he was coming to recognize, they compromised.

"At least give me your shirt and jeans. You can keep your long johns." She added, "I never would have thought you'd be so modest."

"Modest, hell. I'm just afraid we'll have another late-night adventure," he lied, "and I don't want to go dashing out of the house stark naked."

Fiona rolled her eyes. But she felt her cheeks flush with pleasure when his face took on that sleepy, bedroom look he sometimes had and he added, "But if you're willing to take off all your clothes, too, maybe we can renegotiate."

For self-protection, she gave him a look she usually reserved for Brian. "Just toss your clothes out the door when you're done. I'll wake you in a few hours."

She slipped out the door and shut it behind her. Her dogs and cats looked at her hopefully, and she realized she'd been neglecting them.

She pressed her hands to her chest. Her heart was pounding erratically, mocking her brave effort not to think about Eli Becker in her bed in the next room.

Six

"**E**li? Eli, wake up." Fiona opened the bedroom door and crossed the oak floor in her stocking feet. He hadn't responded to her knocking or the sound of her voice. "Eli!"

He grunted grumpily and rolled over, twisting his long legs in the quilt she had given him. He must be very tired, she realized. He had had two hectic days, and this nap was the first time he had slept since arriving at Oak Hill. She pulled back the quilt with the intention of shaking him awake.

She stilled and her mouth curved in a smile of affection. Wearing his waffle-weave long johns and sprawled across her bed, he looked so cuddly and gorgeous. His blond hair was rumpled and curly, the shadow of a beard darkened his lean face and his expression was relaxed.

She felt a sudden yearning to crawl into bed with him, to curl up beside him, to enjoy his warmth and strength. That wasn't all she wanted to enjoy, either, she acknowledged. The clinging fabric of his long johns displayed his leanly muscled build, defining the smoothly bulging lines of his arms, legs, chest, and shoulders. His stomach was hard and flat, and his hips . . .

"Wake up," she said quickly. "Eli, come on. It's time to leave."

He frowned in his sleep. Fiona leaned across the bed and placed one hand on each shoulder. He sighed luxuriously and a slight smile touched his lips. She stared and felt her lips part involuntarily. Then she shook his shoulders and urged him to wake up.

His golden brown eyes lazily opened. He gazed at her for a moment and then murmured, "Fiona. You came."

"I—" Her sentence died on a gasp when he slid his arms around her and pulled her down against his body.

"I thought I was dreaming," he whispered.

He rolled across the bed with her. The world went topsy-turvy for a moment, and then she was lying flat on her back, pinned beneath his heavy warmth. Their eyes locked.

The moment seemed to last forever as she stared into the golden depths of his thick-lashed eyes and felt her breasts heaving against his chest with her suddenly rapid breathing. She could tell the instant he started to wake up because of the confusion that entered his expression. He frowned.

"You're still dressed," he said. "But you were naked a minute ago."

"Not exactly," she croaked.

His gaze dropped to where his arm cradled her head. "I'm in my long johns?" he said incredulously.

"Must have been some dream," Fiona muttered, wishing she had shared it with him.

"It was a dream after all?" Eli groaned in disappointment and lowered his head. He buried his face in her hair and sighed.

She soaked him up. She reveled in the way he felt as he pressed her into the mattress and held her possessively. Then she noticed he had gone very still. "Eli?"

He groaned again. "I know. Midnight watch." He lifted his head and looked down at her again. "I can't believe this. I actually have you in bed, and wouldn't you know it? We're fully dressed, I'm too dead tired to do anything about it, and even if I wasn't, I have to go." He scowled. "Life is so unfair."

He sat up and stretched, drawing the fabric of his long johns tightly across his shoulders. Fiona didn't even try to look away. He yawned and then caught her rapt expression.

"Don't look at me like that," he pleaded. "It just makes it worse."

"You were dreaming about me naked?" she asked curiously.

He grabbed her hand and dragged her toward him, so he could lean over her and stroke her hair. "It's not so surprising. I've been fantasizing about you since we met. My subconscious is just doing its fair share."

His hand slid boldly up her rib cage and closed over a soft breast. He watched as he cupped it, his fingers gentle and massaging. His palm stroked slowly, enticingly across the tight, aching peak, and then his knuckles grazed the valley between her breasts. Fiona could hardly breathe.

"Are you this pretty without three layers of clothing?" he whispered. He put a finger to her lips to still her answer and smiled. "No, don't tell me. It'll be more fun to find out for myself."

They stared at each other for another long moment, full of promise and wonder. Then Eli swallowed and said huskily, "What time is it?"

It took three tries before Fiona could force her voice out of her throat. The hot light in his eyes wasn't making it any easier. "It's almost eleven. Brian said he would stay until you arrived."

Eli helped her sit up. He brushed a soft, burning kiss on her mouth and then said with obvious reluctance, "I've got to go."

Fiona watched him walk out of the bedroom, then pressed a hand to her tingling lips. A moment later he stuck his head back in the room. "Uh, Fiona? Where are my clothes?"

"Kitchen."

"Come watch me dress," he invited, his eyes sparkling naughtily.

"Are you kidding?"

He laughed at her incredulous look. "I guess so. That would really be playing with fire."

She agreed wholeheartedly. She decided to stay safely closeted in the bedroom until he was gone. When she heard him slam the front door behind him, she flopped back on the bed and stared at the ceiling. She groped for the quilt and raised it up to her face. It bore his scent now—golden skin and heavy slumber, male, musky and warm.

She rolled to her side, remembering the graceful way he had rolled across the bed and pinned her beneath him. She would get burned if she let things go any further between them. She knew that. But when she was with him, the flames were irresistible.

Sylvester plodded into the room and dropped his favorite rubber toy noisily on the floor. He wagged his tail and looked at Fiona with hopeful eyes.

"No," she said distinctly. "It's too late. I'm going to sleep now."

He didn't look convinced. He turned out to be right. After an hour of tossing and turning, Fiona finally gave in and played tug-of-war with him. There was no point in pretending to sleep if all she was going to do was think about Eli.

She wished he was in bed with her, touching her again. His admission that he fantasized about her had fanned the fire of her own fantasies, and erotic images were dancing through her mind with a force beyond her control.

She liked having Eli at her dinner table, in her house, in her bedroom. She liked talking to him, looking at him. She wanted to go over to the kennel right now and make sure he was comfortable, that he had everything he needed. But she wouldn't do that. Because she was woman enough to know what would happen between them if she sought him out right now. And she was adult enough to know it wasn't a good idea.

He had made it perfectly clear that he just wanted to wrap up the case and get out of Oak Hill. She didn't intend to get more involved with someone who was going to simply disappear. That would be foolish.

"This is the coolest dog in the world," Brian informed Eli early the next morning.

Eli watched Brian with bleary eyes and tried to look interested. Where the hell was Fiona? She said she would be at the kennel by seven o'clock, and it was nearly eight. Ginny had already spoken to her on the phone, so he didn't even have an excuse to call her.

"Watch this," Brian said. He pointed his finger at the Labrador who was sitting in the staff room with them and said, "Bang! You're dead!"

The dog keeled over and lay on the floor with its tongue hanging out.

"That's pretty good," Eli conceded mildly.

Brian petted the dog and gave him a treat. "And that's not all. Watch this." He put his slip leash around the dog's neck and said, "Take yourself for a walk." The dog paraded around the room holding his leash in his mouth. "Is that cool, or what?" Brian demanded of Eli.

"Yeah, but can he do anything useful, like make another pot of coffee?"

"Man, you're going to rot your pancreas with all that coffee," Brian said critically.

"He's right, you know."

"Fiona!" Eli jumped to his feet when she entered the room. He noticed the dark circles under her eyes immediately. "Are you okay?"

"Yes, I'm fine," she said shortly. "I just overslept."

"Hey, do you two want to be alone?" Brian asked suggestively.

"No," Fiona snapped. "Now go find something to do."

Brian shot Eli a "we men have to be patient with our silly women" look and sauntered out of the staff room, taking the Labrador with him.

Fiona turned to Eli. "Did anything interesting happen last night?"

"Not here," he said significantly.

"No disturbances?"

"No prowlers," he amended. He started walking slowly toward her, a lazy smile on his tired face. "But I thought about you all night, and that was pretty disturbing."

She backed away. "Listen, Eli…" She gasped as his hand closed over her wrist and he pulled her against his body. He felt so good. Too good.

"Hmm?" He touched her cheek with gentle fingers and leaned down to kiss her.

"Wait!"

The shrill sound of her voice made him blink.

She took a steadying breath. "I think that in the interests of professionalism and common sense, we should just forget about last night."

He looked dumbfounded for a moment. "You do?"

She nodded emphatically.

He scowled. "And about yesterday, too?"

"Yes."

"That's asking us both to do a lot of forgetting."

"All we have to forget are a few kisses." Eli rolled his eyes, but she rushed on before he could disagree with her again. "So, with that settled, I suggest we both get to work."

She turned on her heel and dashed out of the staff room as if he were a vicious Doberman. Eli watched her go, feeling a mixture of consternation and hurt. He had been fourteen the last time his kisses had made a female decide *not* to get involved with him.

On the other hand, he knew better than to get involved with a client. Maybe he had been wrong to spend the night thinking Fiona should be an exception to the rule. He ran a hand over his face and felt the roughness on his jaw. He needed a shave. And a shower. And about seventeen hours of sleep. *Then* he could figure out what to do about Fiona.

In the meantime, he was going to have to start checking up on some of the people who had threatened Oak Hill within the past few months. That alone would keep him busy all day.

With Eli either tied up on the phone or gone most of the day, the kennel was shorthanded again. Worried about the blizzard which was still heading their way, and the furnace which was still behaving somewhat erratically, Fiona had her hands full. An endless stream of customers piled through the door all day long. Most of them were demanding and impatient, but Fiona was touched when some of their regular customers brought them gifts and Christmas cookies.

Mr. Snyder showed up that day and further complicated Fiona's life. He demanded to know if she had his beloved Rocky in custody. She saw no reason to lie and admitted that Rocky was staying at Oak Hill. He demanded she release Rocky to him.

"I'm sorry, Mr. Snyder, but we have a contract with Mrs. Snyder guaranteeing that we won't release the dog to anyone but her," Fiona explained quietly, hoping not to attract the attention of the other customers.

Evidently Mr. Snyder didn't feel embarrassed about the custody battle for his dog. "My wife has no legal right to keep that dog from me!" he cried.

"I'm afraid I don't know anything about that, sir. I only know that I'm legally obliged to keep Rocky here until Mrs. Snyder claims him."

"She stole him from me! She snuck off in the night with him, and I've been trying to find him ever since!"

"Would you like to talk somewhere more private?" Fiona asked, realizing that the other customers were listening to Mr. Snyder with open interest.

"No! I want my dog, young woman!"

"Please, Mr. Snyder, there's nothing I can do. Mrs. Snyder could sue us if I released Rocky to you."

She saw by the sly look in Mr. Snyder's eyes that he intended to play his trump card. She braced herself. He signaled to his three sons, who were all standing by the door. They were all thin, pale children. The youngest regarded Fiona with such malevolence that she fell back a step. Mr. Snyder lined them up and stood behind them in a rather sinister family pose.

"Can't you," he purred, encompassing the children in his wistful gaze, "even release Rocky to his true and rightful owners?"

Fiona looked at the three children and swallowed. Aware of being the center of everyone's attention, she said as kindly as possible, "I'm afraid it's just not possible."

Mr. Snyder must have coached the children before arriving. As if on cue, they all simultaneously burst into tears, howling and wailing like the damned.

The uproar was worse than anything Fiona had heard in seven months of living at a boarding kennel. The smallest child pitched his whining voice so high she was certain the windows would shatter in a moment. "Mr. Snyder! Please!" Fiona exclaimed.

Mr. Snyder smirked. Eli walked through the front door at that moment. He cringed at the noise, took one look at the whole scene, and tried to leave again without being caught.

"Eli!" Fiona snapped.

He halted in his tracks, head lowered in defeat, and turned to her with a martyred expression and said, "What's the problem?"

"Mr. Snyder has a black belt in karate. I believe all his children do, too. Maybe you could convince him that I can't legally let him take Rocky out of the kennel," she said nervously.

Eli looked at the Snyder family with bleak eyes. "Can we talk in private a moment, Mr. Snyder?"

In retrospect, Eli was forced to agree with Fiona's assessment that that suggestion had been a mistake. A half hour later, Brian found Eli and Fiona in the lounge. Eli lay prostrate on the couch, cursing, while she tended his wounds.

"Ow! That hurts!"

"Let me take you to the emergency room," she pleaded.

"No!"

"What's going on here?" Brian asked. Fiona saw his face go pale when he looked at Eli. "Good Lord, why's he bleeding again?"

"Eli fell on his head."

"Get that tone out of your voice," Eli snapped.

"Brian, give me a hand, will you?"

"No way."

"Why are men always so squeamish?" Fiona muttered.

"What happened?" Brian asked.

"You should go to the hospital," Fiona repeated to Eli.

"So you and all your pals in the ER can have a few more laughs at my expense? Forget it," Eli snarled.

Recognizing wounded masculine pride and a shattered ego, Fiona decided to let the total unfairness of that remark pass without comment. She bit her lip worriedly and went back to tending the gash on his forehead, hoping her first-aid skills were equal to the task.

"How did this happen?" Brian persisted.

Fiona explained that the Snyders had finally turned up, as Mrs. Snyder had feared, and that she had enlisted Eli's help in making them see reason. "So when Eli got them alone, it was clear they weren't going to be very amenable to reason. In fact, Mr. Snyder is threatening to sue." She shook her head. "He hasn't got a leg to stand on, but we could look very bad if this gets any publicity."

"What I want to know is, when did Eli fall on his head?" Brian said. Eli shot him a look that could have scorched earth.

"Well, when Eli made it absolutely clear we wouldn't release Rocky, Mr. Snyder demanded to at least be escorted into the wings for a brief visit. To see where Rocky was staying and to make sure we were taking good care of him."

"It seemed reasonable enough," Eli muttered defensively.

"Of course it did," Fiona crooned. "Lie still." She finished cleaning the wound and winced when she saw how serious it looked. But she could tell by the stony expression on his face that he wasn't going to change his mind about the hospital. She secretly suspected that he didn't want to fill out those papers about how it had happened.

"So you took him back to see Rocky?" Brian prodded.

"Yes. And they tried to stage a..." Fiona shrugged. "I guess you could call it a rescue attempt."

"They tried to swipe the dog?" Brian asked incredulously.

"Yes. It was all very confusing. There were four of them and two of us, not to mention Rocky. The two older children seized me, Mr. Snyder grabbed Rocky, and the youngest child did this amazing karate leap and kicked Eli right in the—"

"Do you have to tell him that part?" Eli demanded.

"Wow! No kidding!" Brian whistled. "What did you do, man?"

"What I always do when I get kicked there. I turned green and tried not to pass out." Eli closed his eyes in remembered agony. "That kid's feet should be registered as lethal weapons."

"And that's when you fell down?" Brian asked.

"No!" Eli looked insulted. Fiona tried not to laugh, but he caught her choked giggle and scowled again. The poor guy, she thought. It wouldn't do his professional reputation any good to have been successfully attacked by a six-year-old child.

"Then when *did* you fall down?" Brian asked impatiently.

"This may hurt," Fiona cautioned Eli.

"It *already* hurts," he said grumpily.

"I struggled free while the rest of them were all, um, scuffling around," Fiona explained to Brian as she finished patching up Eli. "And I did the first thing that occurred to me. I let Myron out of his run."

Brian's eyes bulged. "You let Myron out? Are you nuts?"

"It was a desperate situation," she said defensively. "Naturally he wanted to join in the fun. He leaped on top of everyone and pretty much put an end to the dognapping attempt. Eli escorted the Snyders out of the kennel and explained why they had better never come back here. And he did it very impressively, too," she added encouragingly.

"Don't humor me," Eli grumbled.

"So when did he fall down?" Brian demanded.

"When we were trying to put Myron back in his run. Myron jumped him. Eli tried to feint to the right, but he slipped and fell down and cracked his head pretty badly, as you can see."

Brian looked at Eli critically. "Man, you are not going to last out the week at the rate you're deteriorating."

"That does it! That *does* it!" Eli leaped to his feet. "I am not going to put up with another minute of this! I am a respected international security expert! Arthur Morgan begged me to leave Naval Intelligence for him! Two heads of state have personally thanked me for saving their lives!" he raged.

Brian looked at Fiona. "Are you sure this guy's stable?"

"He's having a little crisis of confidence," Fiona explained.

"Ever since I got here, I have been hounded by insane animals, crazy teenagers and lunatic customers," Eli continued, warming to his subject. "I'm supposed to be with my family right now, not chasing after phantom prowlers all night and cleaning up after dogs all day!"

"That word *phantom*..." Fiona began.

"But I'm trying," he interrupted. "I'm doing my best, I'm taking this crazy job very seriously, and I'm busting my butt for *your* sake." He pointed accusingly at Fiona. "And all you can do is criticize me and kick me out of bed!"

"I didn't kick you out of bed last night. You left voluntarily," Fiona reminded him.

"You know what I mean!"

"No, I don't!"

"Neither do I. What do you mean, Eli?" Brian asked interestedly.

"I'm just trying to be mature and professional," Fiona exclaimed.

"So am I! But haven't you noticed it's not working for either of us?"

"This is getting good," said Brian.

"Are you finished yet?" Fiona was getting embarrassed.

"No, no, Fifi, let him get it all off his chest," Brian urged.

Eli and Fiona stopped shouting and turned to stare at Brian. Dead silence descended upon the room. Brian folded his arms and smirked. Fiona pursed her lips. Eli ran a hand through his hair and winced.

"I have a headache," he complained.

Fiona resisted the urge to shake him. "I'm not surprised. I think you should go back to my place and lie down for a while."

"No. I have things to do."

"Eli, you can't—"

"I'm not concussed," he assured her.

"But what if—"

"I said I'm okay," he said.

"She *cares*," Brian said mushily. They both glared at him.

Realizing Eli wouldn't relent, Fiona asked, "Did you find out anything today?"

He shook his head. "No likely suspects." He sat down again, moving gingerly now, trying to be kind to his battered and abused body. "If only we could figure out why someone has been coming around here. If only we could figure out what he wants."

Filled with an undeniable urge to comfort and pamper him, Fiona said, "Well, you've probably solved the problem anyhow, Eli, by changing all the locks. Surely once he realizes how futile it will be to attempt entry now...." She shrugged and tried to look encouraging.

"That's only if he was getting in here with a key," Brian said.

"How else would he get in without a trace?" Fiona said.

"Oh, easily," Brian responded dismissively.

Fiona's eyes met Eli's. Then they both pierced Brian with a stern, unblinking stare. Once he had realized his error, he started to squirm. "Go on," Fiona said, not very warmly.

In a blatant attempt to change the subject, Brian said, "Hell, Eli's the security expert. Ask him."

"Fiona and I have already discussed this. But I'd be interested to know how you discovered other means of entry." Eli paused, then added, "And who else knows about this."

Brian shook his head in silent denial. Under Eli's knowing regard he finally admitted, "Well...a few girls."

"A few?" Fiona pounced. "How many equal a few?"

"Oh, that's hard to say."

"Try. Three, four, five?" Fiona pressed.

"More," he said weakly.

"A half dozen? A dozen?" Eli asked.

Brian looked a little ill. "More," he croaked.

"Brian! Just how many girls have you brought here?" Fiona demanded.

"Hey, it wasn't just me, man!"

"What?" she snapped.

"Well, I mean, it *was* in the beginning. But you know, there aren't all that many places for teenagers to go to, uh, get to know each other better." He looked to Eli for sympathy. "Really, it's a big problem in modern society."

"So you told all your friends how to sneak in here with their girlfriends?" Fiona's voice rose to piercing levels.

"Only trustworthy people, I swear!" Brian cried.

"Define trustworthy!"

"Guys like me!"

She looked at him with incredulous, incoherent rage. Then she said the very worst thing she could think of. "I'm going to tell your mother about this."

"No!" he begged. "No! She's already taken a peel off my hide for flunking that class this semester."

"And then I'm going to tell Vicky! And what she'll do to you will make you wish you'd never *seen* a girl!"

"I suspect nothing could have that effect on him," Eli said dryly. "Calm down, Fiona."

"Calm down? Calm *down*? He…he…" When she looked at Eli, she realized that he was smiling. She gaped at him in astonishment before realization dawned. "I was right! You were just like him fifteen years ago, weren't you?"

"Nearly. But I wasn't stupid enough to keep getting caught." Eli's eyes were fairly dancing.

Brian was too distressed to respond to the insult. He just groaned piteously and buried his head in the couch cushions. "My life is over."

"Humph," Fiona said. "So we can assume that half the kids in the county know how to get in here without a key."

"All, probably," Eli said. "I'm sure word spread like wildfire, even among kids who've never actually used the place."

"To think this was all going on right under my nose."

"Please forgive me, Fiona," Brian begged pathetically.

"I can afford to forgive you," she assured him. "Because Vicky and Race will kill you for this."

"Protect me, shield me! Didn't they teach you about mercy in that convent?" he cried.

"You're pushing it," Fiona warned him.

"I hate to break up this diverting scene," Eli said, "but I will need you, Brian, to show me all the ways you taught your friends to break in here undetected. We'll see if we can't block them all off and eliminate yet another possibility."

"Do you realize this means I've wasted all that money on the locksmith?" Fiona demanded.

"No, you haven't. That story you told me about the locks is almost as ridiculous as the story Brian just told us," Eli said rudely.

Brian had the sense not to smirk, but Fiona could tell he wanted to. Eli instructed her to go through her files again to see if anything unusual came to mind, anything that might have bearing on their strange case. He, in the meantime, learned how amazingly and ingeniously devious Brian could be. The kid definitely had a future in espionage, sabotage and subterfuge—once he learned a little finesse.

It was late in the evening before they all finished their respective chores. Fiona had sent most of her exhausted staff home by eight o'clock. In addition to the day's unexpected events, there were nearly two-hundred-fifty animals at Oak Hill now, and everyone was exhausted.

Eli was finishing up a telephone conversation with Arthur Morgan when Fiona found him in the lounge that night. When he saw the golden retriever she had with her, his brows rose. Then he winced as the action caused his forehead to throb.

He touched the gauze bandage there and grimaced. Although he was thankful for Fiona's first-aid skills, he just wished there was one single part of his body that didn't ache. You couldn't seduce a woman—or help her seduce you—if you winced every time she touched you. And he definitely wanted something seductive to happen between them.

He hung up the phone and met her gaze. He gave an inward sigh of regret. Despite their hungry looks during the past few days, his aching body and his professional responsibilities made pleasure pursuits strictly out of the question tonight. The utter weariness in Fiona's face told him that, in any case, tonight wouldn't have been the night.

"That was Mr. Morgan?" she asked, coming to sit near him. The dog trailed after her, an ungainly heap of ears, legs, muzzle, and tail surrounding a slim, still-growing body.

"Yeah. We've gone over the whole situation." He reached over to her to rub a smudge of dust from her cheek. They both silently acknowledged the familiarity of the gesture.

Then Fiona's lashes veiled her eyes and she said, "And he thinks it's all right if you leave tomorrow?"

His chest ached at the way she looked. He suddenly wished she could come with him. "Yeah. He agrees things are at a stalemate at the moment here. If we have another quiet night, it might even mean the whole affair is over." He could see she doubted this. "Anyhow, Arthur will get a couple of kids to pull special duty. One will sleep here at night and the other will watch your house."

"I don't need anybody at my house."

"I want someone protecting you." His tone allowed no argument. If the prowler returned, he was more concerned about Fiona's safety than whether or not the kennel was breached again. The only reason he was willing to leave for even a couple of days at the moment was because there was no reason whatsoever to suppose she was in danger. The one time she had apparently encountered the prowler, he had run away from her and her useless dog.

Fiona shrugged dispiritedly. Eli was leaving. That was all she could absorb at the moment. "Whatever you say."

He waited for her to say something else. He couldn't stand to see her looking so depressed. He covered her hand with his and squeezed gently. "Look, I'll leave my phone number in Wisconsin with you in case anything happens."

She nodded.

"Don't worry. I'll be back before you know it."

Her eyes flashed up to his face in surprise. "You're coming back?"

He blinked. "Of course I'm coming back."

"You never said you were coming back."

"Did you think I'd just desert you?" She practically winced in response. He laced his fingers through hers. "Look, I thought we'd gotten past that. I know I was reluctant to take the job, but things are different now."

"Are they?" she asked doubtfully.

"Yes, dammit! I promised you I wouldn't let anything happen to you and Oak Hill, didn't I?" His insides were hurting as much as his outsides, aching with feelings he could hardly contain. "I'm seeing this through to the end."

Fiona smiled, her expression soft and sad. Yes, he would see the case through to the end. She was learning that much about his integrity, and she believed he wouldn't let her down. Not professionally, anyhow.

"You don't look . . . very happy about that," he said hesitantly.

She decided to change the subject before she got in any deeper. "I brought you a dog."

He accepted her step back onto more neutral ground. "Is this the golden retriever that got dumped on you?"

"Yes. You look so tired, I think you should keep him with you tonight. If you doze off, he'll let you know if anyone tries to break in."

"You're sure about that?" Eli doubtfully eyed the friendly, clumsy dog.

"Oh, I'm sure." She smiled and handed the leash to Eli. "You'll hear him trying to play with the guy."

Eli scratched the dog's ears. It leaned against him and said, "Whooh-oooh-oooh." Eli laughed and thumped its side. The dog made a gurgling noise and wagged its tail.

"If you think you can con me into adopting him, you're wrong," Eli warned Fiona.

She sighed. "I know."

The weary acceptance of her tone bothered him. He took her hand again as she rose to leave. "Will you stay a little longer? Just keep me company?"

He could see she was tempted, but she finally shook her head. "I've got to feed my dogs. And we should both try to get some sleep."

"At least let me walk you home."

"A couple of the girls are almost done locking up. I'm going to double-check everything, and then they'll walk me to my cottage."

"When I get back and all my body parts are in working order, you won't be able to avoid me so easily," he warned.

He was glad to see that familiar teasing light enter her eyes. She batted her lashes at him and said, "We'll see."

Just before she disappeared out the door, he called, "Fiona?"

"Yes?"

"What's his name?"

"The dog? Bundle."

"Bundle?" He regarded the leggy, oversize animal. "That's not very fitting."

"It was a few months ago," Fiona retorted. "Before his owner decided to dump him."

Seven

―――――

"**B**ang! You're dead!" Eli said.

Bundle whined and wagged his tail.

"That's pretty good," Eli said encouragingly. "Now just try to fall over and stop breathing."

Bundle barked and licked Eli's hand.

"I am in awe of your natural ability to train animals," Fiona said dryly.

Eli whirled to face her. It was late morning, and he was in the staff room with Bundle. "He's just a little slow on the uptake, that's all," Eli explained. He held the receiver of the telephone against his ear, hopefully awaiting the voice of an airline employee.

"Got your seat booked?" Fiona asked. She avoided his eyes by stooping down to pet Bundle. Bundle rolled over on his back and waved all four long legs in the air.

"Arthur pulled a few strings," Eli admitted. "I'm just trying to get it confirmed."

"When are you leaving?"

"Tonight." Eli grabbed onto Fiona's curly ponytail and gently hauled her to her feet, then tilted her head back to force her to meet his gaze. "Will you stop looking like that?" he chided gently, feeling guilty. "How many times do I have to tell you I'll be back?"

Fiona knew she was probably being unreasonable. Some people really did come back, after all. Maybe Eli was one of them. She drowned in the golden-brown softness of his eyes and tried to think of something mature to say. All she came up with was, "Tonight? Then you can be here for our Christmas party this afternoon." Her voice sounded too forlorn to fool anyone, least of all Eli Becker.

A tender light entered his eyes. He murmured, "Oh, Fiona, how do you make such a marshmallow out of me?"

She felt her body soften and she leaned against him. Her lips parted, and she stared in fascination at the vibrant, strong angles of his expressive face.

Still holding the telephone, he leaned down slowly. Just before their lips met, he said, "Where's Brian?"

Fiona chuckled and felt the soft puff of their mutual laughter mingle and mix between them. "I sent him out back to check some drains."

Eli relaxed and slid his good arm around her waist. He drew her up with easy strength and kissed her with gentle ardor. His lips met and mated moistly with hers, kiss after kiss, whetting her appetite for something stronger and deeper. Fiona sighed and pressed herself closer to him, fitting her hips against his, letting him know how much more she wanted from him.

Eli groaned and pressed hot, intimate kisses along her smooth cheek and jaw. "This is how it should be between us," he whispered.

She murmured her agreement and started to nuzzle his neck, but her face bumped into the telephone receiver he still cradled there. She pulled back in surprise, but his mouth was on hers again an instant later, and the soft flutter of his tongue could have made her forget anything. She slid her arms around his waist and opened her mouth to his sweetly tickling invasion.

Their tongues tangled together silkily, promising and exciting, teasing and willing. Fiona entwined her fingers in Eli's golden hair and rubbed her breasts against the hard contours of his chest. The muffled sounds of pleasure he made in his throat gave her a thrill of feminine power and mystery. The trembling touch of his bandaged hand on her breast a moment later told her how excited he was, how much *she* excited him, and nothing in her life had ever made her feel so special. Then she gasped and trembled too when he brushed his fingertips across the center of her breast again and again, drawing it into an aching peak.

"Why are you always wearing so many clothes when we do this?" he demanded breathlessly.

She smiled and rubbed her forehead against him like a cat.

"Is that good?" he asked against her hair.

"You can tell it is." Her voice was wispy and strained. Her heart started thudding against her ribs when she felt him fumbling at the hem of her sweater, seeking access to her skin under her layers of clothing. She slid her hands down his sides and around his back, straining against the heat of her anticipation.

"Yes," he whispered. They kissed again, deeply and demandingly, their mouths rough and hungry.

"Mr. Becker? Mr. Becker, are you there?"

They heard the nasal, tinny voice at the same instant. Fiona opened her eyes and stared in confusion for a moment. Then she realized the voice was coming from the telephone receiver which was slowly, inexorably sliding down Eli's arm.

Eli lowered his head for a moment in that familiar gesture of exasperation, then he rolled his eyes at Fiona and held the receiver up to his ear. His other arm tightened around her when she started to draw away. "Yes?" He listened for a moment, then said, "Great. That's all I wanted to know." After he hung up, he added, "But your timing leaves something to be desired. Now, where were we?"

Fiona stiffened and avoided his kiss. "Your flight's been confirmed?"

"Yes. Have I told you that I love the way you kiss?"

"Have a nice trip, Eli." She abruptly pulled herself out of his embrace and turned to leave the room.

"Now what?" he demanded.

"Nothing. I have work to do."

"Fiona…" But she was gone. Eli looked around the room as if searching for a clue to the scene that had just taken place there. His eyes met with Bundle's, who lay on the floor. The dog immediately leaped up and came over to him, eager for affection or dog biscuits, whichever came first.

Eli fished into the pocket of his denim jacket and pulled out one of the biscuits he had learned to always keep with him at Oak Hill. He gave one to the dog and watched him chew. Wouldn't it be nice, he thought, if all his own desires could be satisfied by a quick nosh and a pat on the head?

Right now, Fiona seemed to like the dog better than she liked him. He sighed. "So, Bundle, tell me what you know about women."

Bundle burped and pawed at him, begging for another biscuit. Eli didn't think that technique would work, not even with a woman as eccentric as Fiona.

Since it was Christmas Eve, the kennel would close early that day. The staff party was planned for the afternoon, and Fiona wanted to get all the work done during the morning so that everyone could simply relax and enjoy themselves for a couple of hours right after closing. So she wasn't in the mood for any of Brian's nonsense.

"I'm telling you, I've never seen anything like it. Rocky's got to be moved, Fiona," he insisted. "It's going to take hours to sterilize his run."

It was with great reluctance that Fiona let Brian draw her away from the feeding and medications charts to go take a look at little Rocky Snyder's dog run. Once she saw it, however, she was finally forced to accede to Brian's request.

"You're right," she admitted. "Not even a fraternity boy could live in that mess. All right, I'll move him right away. And you," she added sternly, "had better do a very thorough job of sterilizing this."

"Why don't you call Mrs. Snyder at her emergency number and see if she can get a friend or relative to take him off our hands?" Brian suggested. "He and his family have already caused more trouble than they're worth."

Fiona stared at Brian. Her jaw dropped. Her eyes grew round with horror.

"Fifi! What is it? Are you all right?" he exclaimed.

"Yes, yes," she murmured, wandering away from him on unsteady legs. "Thank you, Brian. That's a very good idea." That she hadn't thought of it before Brian, was an alarming sign of just how much she was losing her grip.

She knew she was tired and overworked. Some of it was the natural result of running the kennel alone during the holidays, and some of it was her overzealous desire to do a good job during Vicky's first absence since hiring her. Naturally the strain of a mysterious intruder had added to her mental fatigue. And the knowledge that Christmas Day was only a few hours away didn't help her emotional condition, either.

But she realized with a sense of great uneasiness that her deficiencies on the job were really due to her obsession with Eli. She turned every corner hoping to see him. She spent every other thought on him, hoping he was comfortable, wondering if his injuries were troubling him, wishing he would stay, wanting him to comfort her as much as she wanted to comfort him, reliving his kisses and embraces and evocative caresses, thinking about what they would say to each other next.

And she knew that that wasn't a good sign at all. She owed it to her job to stop concentrating on him. She owed it to herself to stop daydreaming about a man who would be gone in a few hours. Even if he returned, he would only stay until he had discovered the source of Oak Hill's mysterious problems.

Fiona worked with ruthless efficiency the rest of the day. She fiercely suppressed the rush of pleasure she felt every time she saw Eli and stoically ignored his attempts to please her by teasing her, sympathizing with her, or helping out with the work. She did her best to avoid him all day, even as the staff gathered in the lounge for their annual Christmas party.

Everyone placed their presents under the tree, then helped themselves to the food and drink Fiona had ordered from a local caterer. She wanted to finish her paperwork before she relaxed, and she joined the party a little late.

As soon as she walked into the lounge, she turned down the blaring stereo system and glared at Brian. "Why did I put you in charge of the music this year?" she wondered aloud.

"Hey, man, that stuff was banned, and I'm just doing my part to exercise my constitutional rights."

"Who banned it?" she countered. "Other musicians?"

Brian gave up the argument and helped himself to some more food. Fiona announced that they had broken last year's record and at that moment had the greatest number of boarders in Oak Hill's brief history. She was still worried about the blizzard, though. The weatherman was still making dire forecasts, and the sky looked dark. The wind was pushing heavy black clouds across the sky with increasing speed, and the trees were swaying dramatically just outside the windows.

"Think your plane will really leave in this weather?" Brian asked Eli.

Eli shrugged noncommittally. He didn't want to think about it, because it was too confusing. He wanted to go, he wanted to stay. He didn't want to leave Fiona behind, and he knew she couldn't come with him. He wanted to be with her, yet he didn't want to disappoint the family he hadn't spent Christmas with in ten years. And the harder Fiona tried to be stoic about his leaving, the more he dreaded disappointing her, too.

On the other hand, he was hurt and angry that she didn't believe he would fulfill his obligations to her precious kennel.

He and Arthur had gone over it half a dozen times. It was actually Arthur's decision that Eli should leave and let the kids look after things for a couple of days. Why didn't Fiona believe he would be back in just two days? Didn't she feel how much things had changed between them? Didn't she know how he felt?

He realized with a start that even *he* didn't know how he felt. He only knew that his feelings were zinging wildly out of control inside of him, making him possessive, irrational, and temperamental. He only knew that he had never felt like this before.

They all heard a sudden clanging overhead.

"What's that?" Eli asked.

"Heating system," Ginny answered with a frown. "I thought the furnace man fixed everything."

"He says he did," Fiona said uneasily. "He was here for two hours yesterday afternoon."

"Let's open our presents!" Nadine insisted, attracting everyone's attention.

They had drawn names at Thanksgiving, and each staff member had bought one gift for someone else. Vicky and

Race had left behind gifts for everyone, as well as bonus checks for the permanent staff. Fiona felt a lump form in her throat when she saw the size of her Christmas bonus. The message inside the card told her how much her presence this year had meant to Vicky and Race. She blinked rapidly a number of times, willing herself not to get all mushy and sentimental.

The staff's various gifts to each other were cause for everything from hilarity to heartfelt thanks. Fiona's cheeks reddened with consternation when Brian slyly informed her he had drawn her name and handed her her gift—the sexiest, most revealing negligee she had ever seen. Fiona had drawn Nadine's name and gave that woman a selection of the psychedelic hair dyes, gels and glitters that she favored so much.

Fiona was astonished when Ginny announced that the staff had all pooled together to buy Fiona an additional gift to show her how much they had appreciated her hard work during her first year at Oak Hill. Speechless with emotion, Fiona unwrapped the enormous flat package while everyone watched.

Eli was happy to see Fiona getting the approbation from her staff that she certainly deserved and that he suspected she secretly wanted, too. He felt a surge of pride for the good job she had done under pressure, and for the way these people looked up to her and turned to her again and again during the course of a day. He didn't even question feeling proud of her accomplishments. He only knew it was right and natural.

The gift Fiona unwrapped was a large, beautifully framed print of four collies in a pastoral setting, standing together and looking wistfully into the distance. Each dog was so individual and distinct that Eli thought the artist must have painted the portrait of someone's real and well-loved pets. It would look perfect hanging in Fiona's living room.

Eli smiled softly when Fiona started to thank her staff. He was touched by what they had done, for the framed print was a carefully chosen gift and had surely been expensive, and he could see that Fiona was deeply, sincerely moved. Her voice choked off and tears slipped down her cheeks. He wanted to go to her, to hug her and care for her, but he also wanted her to have this moment to herself. So he stayed where he was. But when her eyes met his across the room, he smiled at her with all the warmth and tenderness he felt and nodded encouragingly. She smiled back, finished her thanks, and wiped her tears away with slim, elegant hands.

It wasn't long, however, before the weather broke up the party. Brian called everyone's attention to the first few snowflakes falling outside the window. Within minutes the flurries had escalated to heavy snowfall. Fiona sent everyone home who wasn't on duty, lest they should get stuck at the kennel as the storm worsened—which the weatherman said it would. Everyone who remained got back to work.

"If you're going to leave, you should go now," Fiona warned Eli. "If there's any accumulation, these country roads won't be fit to drive on." Now that the party was finished, her heart ached even more at the thought of his leaving. Her Christmas celebration was already over, and she would be alone without him.

Eli couldn't fathom the ambivalence inside himself. Now that she was calmly urging him to go, he felt perversely rejected and wanted to stay. He suspected her insanity was starting to rub off on him. "There's no point in going to the airport if the planes are grounded."

"But even if they're not, you might still get stuck out here," she argued.

"If I get snowbound, that'll mean the storm is so bad no one will be flying anyhow."

"But—"

"Will you just let me worry about my flight, Fiona?" he said more irritably than he had intended. Hell, *he* didn't know why he wasn't doing the sensible thing, so how could he explain it to her?

Fiona meekly accepted his flare of temper, aware that he must be terribly disappointed. The darkening sky and heavy snowfall made it seem unlikely that he would be with his family for Christmas this year. And she knew she was the real cause of that.

When Eli saw her nod and quietly walk away, he felt like a heel for snapping at her. She was facing another crisis, and he wasn't helping by being rude to her. He decided to go apologize to her, but Brian handed him a shovel and dragged him outside. The rest of the afternoon was so exhausting and unpleasant that Eli willfully banished conscious thought while he worked.

Just before dark, Fiona decided that the remaining staff should go home immediately. Brian proved his worth, as he occasionally did, by sincerely offering to stay, but Fiona refused.

"We don't know how much worse the storm will get. You could be stuck here," she said.

"What if it's so bad no one can get in to help you tomorrow?" Brian countered. "You'll be alone here with two-hundred-and-fifty hungry animals."

"Not quite alone," Eli reminded him.

Brian's gaze flickered over him dismissively. "An all-American top-ten Kennel worker you're not, Eli."

"It's supposed to clear up by morning," Fiona said, forestalling a typically pointless argument between the two men. "The worst that will happen is we'll get a late start." She calmly met Brian's doubtful gaze.

Finally he sighed and gave in. It was only after he and the others had left that Fiona realized the import of Eli's words. "You're staying?" she asked suddenly.

He nodded. "I called an hour ago. My flight's been canceled. Even if it wasn't, I wouldn't drive all the way to National in this." He glanced out the window where the dark night raged with a howling, disorienting blizzard. "I called Art, too, and told him not to let the kids from the agency risk their necks driving out here from the city. I'll be with you."

Fiona's heart filled with genuine, honest sympathy. She had brought him here against his will, and now he was stuck here on Christmas Eve. Stuck with her when he wanted to be with his family, with the people who nurtured him, cared about him and wanted to share this time with him.

She reached up to touch the square gauze bandage covering the wound on his forehead, then moved her fingertips down to his smooth, lean cheek. She felt his firm, warm skin, saw the sudden darkening of his brown eyes, and her mouth went dry. "I'm sorry," she whispered. "If it weren't for me—"

"Don't say that," he growled.

He was kissing her before he had even realized he intended to. He tightened his arms around her small frame and slanted his mouth hungrily over hers, thrusting his tongue deep inside to savor the taste of this woman who filled his thoughts and dreams, who tickled his heart and tormented his senses.

If it weren't for her... He shuddered. If it weren't for her, he wouldn't be on fire with the hottest, most uncontrollable desire he'd ever known. He wouldn't fill with tenderness to see her smile or cry. He wouldn't rage with wounded pride because he had fumbled like a clown instead of proving to be her knight in shining armor. If it weren't for her, he wouldn't feel so ready to shatter into a million pieces.

She clung to him with the strength that had so amazed him before. She answered his kisses the way he had dreamed she would, with the hunger he craved to feed his own needs. She smelled impossibly sweet and womanly after a day of hard labor, she felt soft and sexy and—

An explosion made them both jump and clutch at each other to keep from falling. A series of gurgles and clangs followed the noise.

"What the hell is that?" Eli exclaimed.

Fiona's face fell. She made a little sound of despair.

"Fiona?" he prodded urgently as more sounds splintered the air.

"It's the furnace," she groaned. "How can this be happening to me?"

"All right, let's stay calm," he said. "Take me to the furnace room."

"Why?"

"Because we can't just stand here and wait for it to explode," he said reasonably.

"No," she said unreasonably. "I don't want to see it. I don't want to know. I can't handle this."

"Come on, Fifi, pull yourself together." He grabbed her hand and started dragging her toward the source of the noise.

"Don't call me Fifi," she said automatically. She trailed behind him slowly, trying to put off the inevitable. The steaming, smoking mess they found inside the furnace room confirmed her worst fears. It would have to be turned off until they got the repairman to come back out.

The rest of the evening was a frantic nightmare. Having turned off the furnace, Eli and Fiona had to find a way to keep all of Oak Hill's boarders warm in the middle of a raging blizzard.

By some miracle, the electrical power didn't fail, so they were able to set up a series of small electrical heaters throughout the kennel wings. When they had used up all of those, Fiona removed all of the blow dryers from the grooming room and set those up in the wings, too.

Then she and Eli went through the entire kennel numerous times, distributing rugs, blankets, and towels to every dog, cat, rabbit and bird to help them stay warm enough.

When they ran out of supplies, Fiona and Eli went back to her house and, under the watchful eyes of her numerous pets, stripped her house of blankets, rugs, quilts, and couch covers. After distributing these, they walked around the wings for two hours, rubbing little paws and tails to keep them warm.

Fiona spent every spare moment on the telephone, trying to find someone to come out immediately to fix the furnace. However, not only was it Christmas Eve, it was also snowing so hard that the few people she got ahold of refused to budge from their homes until the storm was over.

By midnight, Eli decided they had done all they could for the time being. Fiona looked so cold and pale he was worried about her, so he built a fire in the previously unused fireplace in the lounge and insisted she come sit by it.

Fiona protested at first, but he convinced her that she was doing all she could and had to take some time to look after herself if she was going to be of any use the following day.

As the blazing fire warmed her, Fiona removed her bulky winter parka and closed her eyes. Weariness overwhelmed her, and she felt the need to be cared for, protected, cherished. A few moments later she felt the touch of Eli's hand on her bent head. She raised her face to him, sensing the source of strength that could renew her. He gently brushed her dark hair away from her face and handed her a steaming mug of hot chocolate. A moment later he pulled off his boots and sat beside her on the couch.

"Of all the Christmas holidays I've spent in strange places," he said, "of all the nights in my life when duty took precedence, I've never done anything as wholly unexpected as this."

Fiona smiled at the rueful, teasing note in his voice. "Nothing has gone as planned this year," she admitted.

"It's a lot to handle, your first time alone."

Fiona hesitated for only a moment, then reached for his hand and squeezed it. "But I'm not alone. You're here with me. If it weren't for you, Eli, I don't know how I would have survived the past six hours. Thank you."

Eli met the soft yearning of her sea-colored gaze and forgot what he had intended to say next. The dim lights and blazing fire shone on her thick chestnut hair and made her fair skin look translucent. Her lips looked soft and appealing, and when her pink tongue flicked out to wet them, he felt something shatter inside him.

Fiona felt the shudder that made Eli's hand tremble for a moment, and she drew in a sharp breath. *This is it,* she thought suddenly. *Last chance to run.* But even as he pulled her slowly, inexorably toward him, inch by inch, breath by breath, she knew that she had lost her last chance to run away from him days ago.

She placed a hand on his hard chest to brace herself, and she could feel the powerful beat of his heart, could feel his body heat burning through layers of wool and soft flannel. The dynamic sexual tension which had suddenly seized him was apparent in the rigid, waiting stillness of his muscles, in the sudden shallowness of his breath, and in the way his eyelids drooped heavily and his thick lashes veiled the golden gleam in his dark eyes.

He placed his hands around her small waist and lifted her against him so she straddled him as he leaned back on the couch. Her breasts pressed teasingly into his chest, and his thighs rested intimately between hers.

She could feel him looking at every inch of her body: her face and hair, her neck and shoulders, her breasts which rose and fell with her unsteady breaths, her taut stomach and narrow waist, and her thighs, which had convulsively tightened on his with hungry longing.

The dark gold of his hair caught and teased the firelight, gleaming fluffy and soft, inviting the touch of her fingers. She lowered her eyes and admired everything she had already noticed about him. His whole body was strong and hard and lean, slim and big boned and graceful. His bruises and bandages made him look like a wounded hero. He smelled like her fantasies, moved like her dreams, looked like her deepest longings and felt like her darkest desires. And now he was inviting her to touch and explore him, to test every one of her erotic visions on his living flesh. Fiona shivered.

Eli's eyes flew up to her face. "Are you cold?" he whispered.

"Yes. No. I don't know." She brushed her fingertips across his warm lips. "Eli . . ."

He kissed her fingers, then brushed his wet, silky tongue back and forth against them. He smiled at the tiny sound of arousal she made, then slid his hands into her hair and pulled her face closer to his.

"Listen to me," he murmured.

"I'm listening." She strained against his hold, trying to touch her mouth to his. She could feel the sweet heat of his breath against her lips and the tickle of his hair on her forehead, but he held her fast for another aching moment.

"This isn't exactly what I had planned for our first time together," he growled, "but right now I don't care."

Since her voice was stuck in her throat, she simply shook her head to show she agreed with him.

"We're going to make love," he breathed against her lips. He took a quick, biting kiss and pulled back again. He was breathing harder. "I don't care if the sky caves in and the whole damn kennel tumbles into the river, we're making love now and nothing else matters. Got that?"

She nodded, wishing he would shut up and get on with it. When he released his hold on her hair a moment later, she sank against him and sought the soul-destroying power of his kiss.

His lips were hot and demanding, hungry and exploring. His arms held her so close that his heartbeat thundered through her senses and his deep, ragged breathing became the sound of her own sighs. He devoured her, and she gave herself up freely to his hunger, opening her lips to the fierce probing of his tongue, offering the hidden heat of her mouth to his questing fervor.

He tasted like everything she had ever longed for in the lonely nights and brave-faced days of her life, like love and affection, like friendship and passion, like need and fulfillment. She answered every caress and made demands of her own. *Need me, love me, stay with me.* The feverish, almost painful grip of his hands on her body seemed like the answer she sought from him.

She was burning in his heat, drowning in the flood of their mutual desire, floating without weight in the dark, tumultuous whirl of his passion, reveling in the frantic roughness of his hands as he fumbled to get under the layers of wool, flannel, and cotton that protected her...

"Arrrrgh!" She screamed and shot straight up.

Eli took hold of Fiona's shoulders and demanded, "What? What is it?"

"Your hands are like ice," she choked out.

They stared at each other for a moment, gasping for air, and then they started laughing. He pulled her back against him and hugged her. "What can I warm them on, I wonder?" he murmured suggestively.

"Yah! Not there," she pleaded, squirming.

"Mmm. Too bad." He nuzzled her hair and pressed lazy kisses along her neck while his hands slid around her body and his nimble fingers worked on the unseen fastenings of her clothing. "Here?"

"That's...um...*oh*." Fiona bit her lip and squirmed a little closer to him.

"Let me just unhook... Ahhh. Comfortable?"

She nodded her head and sighed.

"They're nice and warm," he whispered. She gasped when he cupped his palm and squeezed gently. He kissed her and added, "*Very* nice."

Fiona slid her arms around Eli's neck and rested her forehead against his while his hands teased and admired her. He brushed the smooth slopes with his knuckles and explored the full curves with his palms. He teased the tender nipples with his fingertips then pinched the aching peaks. Fiona moaned and moved restlessly on his lap.

"What color are they?" he whispered against her ear.

"I'm not telling," she murmured, wanting him to look at her despite the chill air.

He smiled and eagerly raised the hem of her sweater. "Hold this," he ordered. Then he pulled up her flannel shirt, her T-shirt, and her waffle-weave underwear, and he shifted aside the bra he had already unhooked. "This is like hunting for buried treasure." He touched her leisurely. "You're hot now."

"Hmm-mmm," she sighed.

"Pink," he said huskily. "Perfect coral pink, and small and pretty." His warm hands slid around her back and massaged her for a moment before lifting her slightly.

Fiona arched her back and tilted her head, letting her hair spill backward and her hands rest on his shoulders. She felt the tender kiss of his lips on each hard nipple, and she closed her eyes in ecstasy. He nuzzled her breasts, fanning them with his breath and teasing them with his clever mouth.

When she felt the wet, languid caress of his tongue, she started panting and moaning his name. She felt him licking and stroking, rolling his mouth around her aching nipples, laving them with hungry impatience. She wished she could see his face beneath the bulky lump of her rolled-up sweater, but she was content to close her eyes and melt in the dark mystery of his touch.

Eli took one rosy peak between his lips and sucked, gently at first, then with increasing enthusiasm as Fiona went wild and ran her hands across his back, around his neck and through his hair. His hungry suckling made the ache in her loins unbearable, even painful, and her whole body trembled with a need she had been denying since meeting him.

She made soft little grunting noises and fumbled at his clothes, wanting to touch him, wanting to make him feel this way too. The moment her hand touched the hard, smooth flesh of his belly, she felt it contract as he gasped. Her hands were just as cold as his had been.

"We must be crazy," he muttered, seeking her mouth with his own.

Fiona nodded and spoke between the hot, rough kisses they exchanged, breathlessly telling him, "I wish you could take your clothes off."

"I wish I could take *your* clothes off. But I don't want you to catch pneumonia." He unsnapped her jeans as he spoke.

"But you just said—"

"Fi-ona," he said with a grin, "a *few* things have to come off unless you know a completely new and revolutionary way to do this."

"I suspect you know more ways than I do," she said, as dryly as she could with Eli pulling her zipper down.

He reached across her and said, "Help me spread your coat on the couch."

"Why?" She rubbed her face against his neck and pushed her hands farther up inside his shirt. His chest was muscular and lightly furred. "Is it blond or brown?" she whispered.

"So you can lie on the lining. The couch is almost as cold as the carpet."

"You spread it. I'm busy." She pulled and tugged at his clothes until she satisfied her curiosity. His chest hair was dark, dark gold. He would look beautiful sleeping in the sun. Her rapturous examination was interrupted when he tilted her off his lap and laid her down on top of the warm lining of her coat, which he had struggled to spread while she was admiring his body.

Their eyes locked. His expression was lambent and full of promise. He covered her body with his, warming her all over, and braced his bandaged hand above her head. He slid the other hand inside her unzipped jeans and rubbed her with slow, mesmerizing strokes. Fiona's breath started coming deep and hard.

"You're scalding hot there," he whispered with a pleased smile. They exchanged a long, intimate kiss. He moved his hand lower. "Do you like that?"

"Don't tease me," she pleaded, wanting him to keep on teasing her. Nothing had ever been as delicious as the pressure of his palm against the apex of her thighs.

Then Eli peeled back her long underwear to slip his fingers inside her lacy panties and investigate the wet heat there with bold fingers. Fiona cried out and arched against him. "That's it, honey," he encouraged her, "tell me how it feels."

She clutched at him and writhed excitedly beneath him, responding without thinking to his stroking fingers, wanting more than that, wanting everything he could give. She groped blindly for his belt buckle. When she found it, she undid it as quickly as her trembling fingers would allow, then she cupped her hand over him.

Eli made a growling sound deep in his throat and pushed himself into her gentle hands. "Unzip me," he ordered huskily, breathing as if he had just run twenty miles.

She did as he asked, aware that he winced as she lowered the zipper with rough haste. Then she dipped her hands inside his jeans, closed her fingers around him, and drew him out.

Eli pulled Fiona's pants down her thighs, kissing her and murmuring to her, stopping to touch and admire. Then he lowered his body heavily onto her, shifting and adjusting as she did, sliding his narrow hips between her legs, fitting himself comfortably into the cradle of her thighs.

Everything ignited in Fiona's mind, the quick, sultry kisses Eli spread across her face and neck, the hard press of his belly against hers, the sudden tensing of his body, the way his fingers folded around hers as she guided him to his goal.

Then she felt the hot, hard, invading strength of his manhood, and all her thoughts and sensations focused on that first, slow, piercing thrust as Eli entered her. They both went rigidly still for a moment, then Fiona heard her own breath gusting in and out of her lungs as she breathlessly urged him forward. She wrapped her arms around him possessively and felt him arch his back, then he pushed again and slid his hands under her hips to guide her motions and ease his way.

Fiona gasped as he thrust again, then she arched her back and felt him bury himself to the hilt, as deep inside of her as he could go.

"Oh, Lord, you feel so good, sweetheart," he rasped against her cheek.

"Hurry," she begged.

"No." He kissed her face, her mouth, her hair. "No, I've waited for this since we met. Let's make it last."

Fiona sobbed, since his words only fueled the flames in her body, in her heart, and she wanted him to put it out *now*. She moved her hips against him.

Eli shuddered and stilled her teasing motion with the ruthless strength of his hands. "No fair."

"I don't feel fair," she panted.

But he made her wait, petting her with passion and intimacy, greedily soaking up her kisses and caresses, whispering to her about how good their bodies felt joined together. They were both sweating profusely in the chilly room by the time he gave in to her pleas and cries and started moving against her, with her, into her in the ancient, primitive rhythm that had hummed inside her body since the first time she laid eyes on him.

The flood of consuming pleasure came upon her quickly, pouring, spilling, flowing through her like a tidal wave. She clung to him, aware of every move and sound he made as he gave himself to her, as he used every ounce of her strength to push her over the edge and hold her while she fell. It was only when she was too weak to feel anything else, when her weary body had withstood all the magic it could bear, that she felt him release the tight control he had kept on himself. He drove into her fast and hard, holding her with fierce intensity, straining to breathe as he finally unleashed the last of his needs and trembled with completion, losing himself inside of her.

She held him in his most vulnerable moment, then stroked his hair as he sank against her, weak and content. His hand brushed across her ribs, then found her own hand. He laced his fingers with hers and sighed.

Fiona smiled softly as her eyes closed. Only Eli could have turned this disastrous Christmas Eve into the best night of her life. He always did the unexpected.

"Oh, Eli," she said with a sigh.

He nuzzled her hair but didn't move otherwise. "Merry Christmas, sweetheart."

He fell asleep even before she did.

Eight

———

The cold woke Eli, but despite his discomfort, he was aware of a deep sense of satisfaction. He burrowed against the warm, slight body of the woman lying beneath him, knowing that she was the source of his contentment. She smelled of sleep and woman and the aftermath of love, so he buried his face in her neck, concentrating on the feel of their bellies and loins pressed warmly together, and tried to ignore the cold creeping through him.

When he realized that it wouldn't work, that he was only getting colder instead of falling back asleep, he finally lifted his head. Fiona's face looked peaceful and lovely in the first rays of the morning sun. Eli smiled and pressed his lips to the pale, baby-soft skin of her cheek. Then he realized. Sunlight!

He sat up carefully, trying not to disturb Fiona, and peered over the edge of the couch to look out the window. The sun was shining brilliantly in a crystal-clear sky that showed no trace of yesterday's furious storm. The thick blanket of snow that covered Oak Hill made the sun's radiance seem even brighter. Eli guessed that it was after eight o'clock. He realized with surprise that he and Fiona had slept the whole night through after making love, instead of checking hourly on the animals as they had intended.

He glanced at her sleeping form. She would feel guilty and upset when she realized she'd done so, but she had needed the sleep. As he studied her glowing face, he discovered for the first time what she looked like when she wasn't totally exhausted. He grinned and his heart started thudding heavily.

Then it jumped in alarm when he heard a door slam. His first thought was that it was their phantom prowler at last. Then he realized that it must be some of the staff, arriving late for work due to road conditions.

"Anybody here?"

Eli heard Brian's voice calling through the kennel. A moment later the student shouted again, much nearer this time. Eli rolled to his feet and adjusted his trousers at the same moment Fiona woke up.

"Hello?" Brian called. "Eli? Fifi?"

Fiona blinked in confusion and started to sit up. Eli realized that Fiona's clothing was still arranged to expose everything from her collarbone to her knees. He scooped his denim jacket up from the floor and threw it across her body a bare instant before Brian and his mother entered the room.

"Here you are!" Ginny said.

"Hi, there," Eli said with attempted casualness.

"Urmph," Fiona said, her face going scarlet.

Brian stalked forward in his thigh-high rubber boots and his amazing floppy-eared Tibetan hat. "Man, you should see it out there! It's like a Siberian wilderness!"

Fiona stared at them all openmouthed, so Eli jumped into the breach. "How'd you guys manage to get here?"

"Four-wheel drive," Ginny said.

"And I pushed the damn thing nearly halfway here," Brian added.

"Think anybody else will make it?" Eli asked.

"In about another hour," Brian said. "There are already a few snowplows out there, and there will be more soon. Some Christmas this turned out to be, huh?"

Eli grunted. Fiona peered cautiously beneath the denim jacket he had draped over her, then gasped and clutched it tightly to her body. Brian looked at her with interest.

"What have you two been doing since last we met?" he asked slyly.

"Working our butts off," Eli said quickly. He took Brian and Ginny firmly by the elbow and led them out of the lounge, talking about the collapse of the furnace and the horrid evening that had followed. He left out the night's rapturous conclusion and stoically ignored Brian's speculative glances.

Once alone, Fiona straightened her clothes, tied her hair into a messy ponytail, and went into the kitchen to make a pot of coffee.

She had known exactly what she was doing last night, and she certainly couldn't say she regretted it. But in the cold light of the morning, it didn't look like the most sensible thing she had ever done.

If she closed her eyes, she could still feel the smooth, powerful glide of his hips between her thighs, taste the sweet manna of his kisses on her tongue, hear the rough timbre of his explicit whispers in her ears, remember the tender way he had laced his fingers with hers before falling asleep...

"Are you okay?" he asked softly.

Fiona's eyes flew open. Eli was standing in the doorway watching her. The moment her gaze locked with those lambent brown eyes, liquid heat started pooling in her loins. She could see in his expression that he remembered every detail of last night just as clearly as she did. And he looked as if it was an awfully good memory for him, too.

"I'm okay." Her voice sounded about two octaves lower than normal.

"Do you mind that he knows?"

"*Does* he know?"

Eli's mouth curved wryly and he nodded. "Oh, yes. He's not saying anything in front of his mother, but he knows. I think he knew before we knew."

Since she felt too muddled to follow that line of reasoning, and too vulnerable to ask what would happen now, Fiona took refuge in her duties. She conscientiously thanked Eli for his help, humbly asked if he would mind lending a hand today since they were virtually snowbound anyhow and graciously outlined the schedule she planned for the day. When he courteously agreed to all her proposals, she assumed with relief that she would be able to get through this awkward morning-after feeling without getting singed.

But when she brushed past him to begin her work, he clamped his good hand around her arm. "Wait a minute," he said. "You've forgotten the most important thing."

Fiona looked up into his teasing face and felt her stomach flip over. "What?" she croaked.

"My good-morning kiss," he said seriously. "Make it good, because it looks like we'll be too busy for another if you don't get it right the first time."

"If I don't get it right?" she repeated indignantly. She grabbed his collar and pulled his face down to hers. "Of all the nerve."

She put all of last night's remembered magic into the warm, leisurely kiss she gave him. And if she had to lean against him for a moment afterward, she was pleased to note that his breath was unsteady, too, and his hands were greedy.

"Fiona," he said at last, "there's something we have to talk about."

She tensed. "Yes?"

He cleared his throat. "I'm so ashamed that last night I... Well, that I didn't even take any precautions."

She stared into his concerned face for a moment and then realized which precautions he was talking about. "Against pregnancy?" When he nodded, she relaxed again. "It's all right, I'm on the pill. Believe me, Eli, I of all people would never risk an accidental child."

He gave her a puzzled look. "It's good to know we didn't risk it after all, but why do you say *you* of all people?"

She shrugged and changed the subject again, reminding him that they had a lot of work to do. After another quick kiss, she left him standing in the kitchen, looking after her with a speculative frown.

As Brian had predicted, the rest of the staff came stumbling in one by one, telling harrowing tales about road conditions. Fiona spent the morning harassing various people on the phone, and by noon someone had arrived to repair the furnace. Fiona knew that she'd be charged a small fortune for the work since it was Christmas Day, but the dogs and cats had to have heat. They had all survived the night without incident, despite the fact that Fiona had neglected her responsibility to them, but she didn't intend for them to go through anything like that again.

It was midafternoon by the time the furnace was finally working again. Fiona calmly accepted the repairman's diagnosis, but she didn't stifle Brian when he threatened to sue the company if they had once again failed to repair it properly.

By the time it started getting dark, Fiona realized with surprise that Christmas Day, which she had been dreading for weeks, was nearly over. The challenges and responsibilities of the day had been so awesome, and her thoughts about Eli had been so absorbing, that she didn't give the lonely holiday a thought.

Until Eli called his family.

Fiona had been helping one of the kids put salve on a mean dog's foot, and the experience had so tired her that she decided to retire to the staff room for a quick coffee break.

She found Eli sitting there with Bundle, the abandoned golden retriever, talking to his father on the telephone.

As soon as she walked in he covered the receiver and said, "Don't worry, I called collect."

"I believe you," she assured him, "but you didn't need to. It's the least we could do."

A moment later Eli said, "Yeah, put her on." Judging by the tone of his voice, Fiona guessed that the next person he spoke to was a child. "I know I promised I'd be there, honey, but I was wrong."

Eli listened for a moment, then he grimaced and shifted uncomfortably. "I said that? You're sure it was me?" He ran a hand over his face and considered the child's next statement. "Well, yes, a promise should never, ever be broken. But sometimes, no matter what we do, we can't keep a promise." After another pause, he said, "Your daddy's right. I tried very hard to be with you today." He smiled a moment later. "No, Uncle Eli's not perfect, after all. Just ask Grandma."

There was a terrible sensation in Fiona's chest, like a lead weight pressing down on her and constricting her breath. To hear Eli comforting his niece over his absence made her feel guilty. To listen to how sweetly he spoke to a child started a slow throbbing deep inside her. To think of him belonging to them made her jealous. And that made her ashamed. She took a deep breath and frowned at the mistiness in her eyes.

"Yeah, let me talk to Grandma," Eli said. A moment later, "Hi, Mom. Sorry... I know. Me, too." He shifted the receiver to his other ear and asked his mother about various people. He laughed as he listened to her account of the family's Christmas together. At last he sighed and said, "No, you tell them all for me, it'll be easier. I'll try, Mom. Likewise. I love you, too. Bye." He hung up and stared at the receiver for a moment with a slight smile. Then he looked at Fiona.

When their eyes met, she felt a rush of tumultuous emotions. She wanted to go to him, she wanted to hide from him. She searched for something to say, but only came up with, "I'm sorry."

"It's okay," he said quietly. He petted the dog and looked at Fiona with such steady intensity that she felt her nerves quiver.

"It sounds like you have a big family," she said weakly.

He nodded. "My parents, two sisters, two brothers, four nephews, one niece, and a few in-laws."

"Oh." Fiona nodded.

"Do you have a big family?"

"No."

"That's right. I asked you that once before, didn't I? Well, how small is your family?"

She shrugged noncommittally. The expectant silence lengthened until Fiona felt like wincing. "Just me."

Eli leaned forward and frowned slightly. "You have no family?" he asked softly.

She shook her head. "No." When it became clear that he was prepared to wait till spring for her to expand on that brief response, she cleared her throat and said, "That convent . . . It was really a Catholic orphanage."

Eli petted Bundle but kept his eyes on Fiona. "I wondered why you spent all of Christmas Eve and Christmas Day here without even calling anybody." He let out a gust of breath. "You're an orphan, then?"

Fiona nodded again. "Vicky and Race know, but the kids all think I'm just, um, convent-educated."

"Why the big secret, Fiona?"

"It's not really a big secret. I just . . . don't like the way people act when they find out."

"How's that?"

"They feel sorry for me," she said shortly.

Eli nodded slowly. Fiona's blood was roaring in her ears, but she didn't know why she should be so nervous about telling him or why she was waiting so tensely for his reaction. He just kept thinking and petting the dog.

She was used to all sorts of reactions. Some people asked her with ghoulish curiosity if her life had been like Oliver Twist's. Some expressed an overflow of unbearable pity, while other tried to shrug it off as one of those little annoyances that happened to everybody. Vicky had initially accepted Fiona's story matter-of-factly; after they became friends Vicky had confided to Fiona that her own home had been such that she might as well have been an orphan.

But Eli just sat there thinking and digesting the news. For once his face gave nothing away, and she couldn't tell how he felt or what he thought. She was getting ready to explode when he said quietly, "I'm sorry I've made such a big deal about Christmas with my family ever since we met, Fiona."

Fiona blinked. "Well...it was important to you. They're all there today." Then she frowned. "If you would have changed your behavior just because I have no family... Well, that's exactly the sort of thing I don't need."

"I guess not," he agreed mildly. "But there will be other days." He forgot about all his objections to this crazy job or to breaking his promise to his family. He was just glad that he was here with Fiona when no one else would have been. That was suddenly more important. He shifted, wishing he could get more comfortable with the sensations pulsing through him.

The delicate balance of the atmosphere was broken by a sudden uproar. They heard a door fly open and hit the wall, a chorus of noisy barking, and a lot of screaming, cursing, and thudding.

"Get him!" came a voice from the back hall.

"That's Brian," Eli said, jumping to his feet. Fiona and Bundle followed him out of the room.

Everything happened very quickly after that. Fiona rounded the corner just in time to see a small brown body rush directly between Eli's feet. Eli flew up in the air. Brian made a flying tackle for the dog, and he smashed into Eli instead. The two of them made a desperate attempt to keep their balance, but they flew into a bank of metal shelves, and the cans of dog food stacked there came tumbling down on them.

"Oh, my God," Fiona said despairingly.

It took a while to get their arms and legs untangled and to ascertain that their injuries were superficial. Fiona suspected that Eli had sprained the hand which was still healing from the dog bite, but he cursed and flailed so much she couldn't examine it properly. He couldn't walk without limping, but he wouldn't even discuss that with her. Men were so absurd, Fiona thought crossly.

When Brian recovered enough to move around, he said, "We've still got to catch Houdini before he finds a way out of here!"

"Who the hell is Houdini?" Eli snarled.

"He's a regular boarder," Fiona explained. "He's an escape artist."

"Oh, come on," Eli snapped.

"No, man, it's true," Brian said. "That dog has escaped from this kennel four times. No other dog has ever escaped even once, but he does it practically every time he comes here. It's, like, uncanny. And Fiona," he added with a fierce glare, "put him in my wing yesterday."

"We'd better find him," Fiona said, ignoring Brian's look of self-righteous outrage.

It took them so long to track down Houdini that Fiona began to fear he had indeed escaped again. When they finally discovered him trying to shimmy up the chimney in the lounge, it took the three of them another ten minutes to seize and subdue him. Despite Fiona's protests, Eli tied Houdini up like a murder suspect and carried him back to Brian's wing. Fiona went with him and showed him which run was Houdini's.

"Wait a minute," Eli shouted above the barking. "Isn't this Rocky Snyder's run?"

"I moved him yesterday at Brian's request. Houdini checked in after we sterilized it."

It took Eli another twenty minutes to untie Houdini and get out of the run without letting the dog out. He was panting with exhaustion and aching with new bumps and bruises by the time he finally flung himself down on the couch in the lounge.

"You're filthy," he said critically to Fiona.

"So are you," she snapped back. "Will you just hold still for minute?" She yanked on his soot-covered hair so she could examine him.

"You aren't a doctor," he growled.

"Then I suggest we go to the emergency room where—"

"No!"

"Will you two just shut *up* for a second?" Brian pleaded.

Feeling somewhat chastened for bullying an injured man, Fiona meekly accepted this rebuke. The three of them were covered with ashes and cinders from the fireplace. Ginny came into the lounge and clucked maternally over Brian. Fiona gave up trying to tend Eli and started cleaning up the mess around the fireplace.

"We'll have to get the carpet cleaner in here after Christmas," she muttered. "Make sure you lock that dog in *good* tonight, Brian."

The rest of the day was mercifully routine. They all finished their final duties, did the last of the laundry, and locked up the kennel. After Fiona had sent the rest of the staff home that night, she found Eli holding his aching head in his hands. She smiled and brushed his sooty hair off his bandaged forehead.

"Why don't you come back to my place?" she invited. "You can take a shower and relax. I'll even cook you dinner."

His eyes sparkled tiredly as he pressed a kiss into her palm. "I want you to do more than cook for me."

She smiled wickedly. "I want you to taste more than my food."

"Oh, Fiona," he sighed, pulling her down onto his lap. "You almost make me forget that I feel ready to be buried."

"Come on," she urged. "You'll feel better after you clean up and eat."

They put on their coats and walked hand in hand back to Fiona's cottage. For the first time since arriving at Oak Hill, she became fully aware of how romantically beautiful the oak grove was.

"I walk through here every day," she said as they strolled beneath snow-laden branches, "but tonight it looks like a fairy-tale setting."

"It's because you're with me," Eli said modestly. He tugged on her mittened hand to stop her and turned her to face him. He slid his arms around her. "Has anyone ever told you you look like a love goddess in the moonlight?" He placed his gloved fingers over her mouth. "No, don't answer. Let me pretend it's an original line."

She laughed at him and tasted the salty leather of his glove. Eli made a little sound and kissed her, a passionate graceful kiss full of magic and moonlight.

"I wanted it all to be like this," he murmured regretfully. "I wanted to be smooth and brave and heroic for you. Instead, I got bitten by a dog that *you* had to rescue me from, beaten up by a six-year-old, clobbered by a Saint Bernard and today I looked like a Keystone Kop."

"No, you—"

"The only person I've successfully defended you from was Brian the night he arrived, and I wound up feeling like a jerk then, too."

Fiona smiled tenderly and touched his cheek with her mitten. "I haven't exactly been a good damsel in distress," she reminded him.

He grinned. "No, I guess not. But you've been everything a woman needs to be." They kissed again, their arms tight around each other, their lips tender and pliable. "Let's go home."

Fiona nodded, and slipped her arm through his as they continued on their way, her head resting comfortably on his shoulder. When they reached her house, she sent him into the bathroom while she tended to her dogs. She showered quickly after Eli, then prepared dinner while he sat at the kitchen table and watched her.

"I'm afraid this isn't much of a Christmas feast," she apologized as she placed spaghetti and meatballs before him. "Off! Off!" she said to a cat who had jumped onto the table and was curiously sniffing Eli's dinner. Fiona clapped her hands sharply. "Everybody out! Come on, Sylvester. You, too." When the last of her pets had plodded out of the kitchen—after bestowing a reproachful look on Fiona—she closed the swinging door and bolted it in place.

"Alone at last," Eli said dryly as Fiona sat down to dinner with him. They ate hungrily, talking only a little. Eli didn't broach the subject of most interest to him until after dinner, when they were sitting in the living room, drinking Irish cream liqueur and enjoying a cozy fire with Fiona's shaggy family.

"Do you know how you wound up in an orphanage?" he asked abruptly.

She tensed. He wondered for a moment if she would change the subject, but at last she met his eyes and said, "I was abandoned when I was seven."

Eli's eyes widened. Shock coursed through him, and then her answer settled into place inside him. He realized instantly how important those words were. And he wanted to know the whole story. He scooted closer to her on the rug before the fireplace and tried to obliterate any sign of emotion from his voice, lest she misinterpret it as pity, as he asked, "What happened?"

She didn't normally talk about it. There was no real need for him to know, and sleeping with her didn't give him the right to insist she tell him. So she supposed she answered him because, for some reason, she wanted him to know. "One day my mother took me to church. She put me in a pew and told me to stay there till she came back for me. I was afraid to stay there alone, but she promised me she would be right back and told me not to worry about it."

Fiona took a deep breath and stared into the fire, remembering. "She gave me a letter and told me to keep it with me. I could still barely read, so I didn't know what it said. She left then. I waited." She picked up Tidbit and petted her absently. "I waited for what seemed like a long time. People came and went, but my mother didn't come back. Finally, someone noticed me sitting there by myself. The priest came out then and tried to speak to me."

Fiona shrugged. "I guess I must have realized something terrible was happening, because I started crying and wouldn't talk to him. He managed to pull the letter out of my hands. He didn't tell me what it said, and I didn't ask. I could tell by the way he acted that it was bad news."

"Did it— She wrote it to tell the priest she was leaving you in his care?" Eli asked thickly. He could picture Fiona, a little wide-eyed, brown-haired girl, sitting alone in a church and waiting for a mother who would never return.

Fiona nodded. "It was a long, ugly night. Father McCarren didn't tell me I'd been abandoned. He began by saying that I was supposed to stay with the Sisters for a few days. When it stretched out to a few weeks—he was never able to find my mother—he finally tried to explain that I would have to live permanently with them."

"Did you understand any of it?"

"No." She sighed. "It was years before I understood. I thought she had been kidnapped or taken from me. I blamed Father McCarren and thought he was hiding me from her. I blamed the nuns. Then, when I was old enough to realize my mother had left me on purpose, I blamed myself. I did a lot of blaming one way or another.''

"You weren't adopted?''

"No.''

"Why not? I don't mean to sound crass, but you must have been a beautiful little girl. Why didn't anyone want to adopt you?''

She gave him a hard look. "Your parents had five children. Were any of them adopted?''

"No,'' he admitted.

"Not many people who can have their own children choose to adopt other people's. And people who do adopt often want babies instead of children. The older an orphan gets, the less likely he or she is to find a permanent home. Knowing what I know now, I also think I was better off with the Sisters than I would have been at a series of foster homes.'' She shrugged. "Anyhow, for the first few years I was at the orphanage, I was an extremely unpleasant little girl. In fact, I was in my late teens before I accepted the facts and decided to get on with life.''

"Was it...at all like a home there?'' He had grown up in such a secure family, he couldn't imagine what she had faced.

"I guess not. We weren't tortured or starved or anything that movies and bad novels would have you believe. I guess it was just like being at boarding school permanently. I was lucky in that a wonderful woman, Sister Mary Elizabeth, took a special interest in me. Lord knows she had enough responsibilities and could never really be like a mother to me, but she tried. I still write to her sometimes. And I had a best friend who was like a sister to me.''

"Where is she now?''

"Massachusetts. She married very young. Mostly to find some stability. But she's stayed with him.''

She said no more, but Eli had the impression that it wasn't exactly a strong marriage. "And what did you do?''

"I studied hotel management. There was a good opportunity for me, thanks to Father McCarren, and I figured that way, I'd always have a place to live." She smiled without much humor. "It was a real shock when my last hotel job told me I'd have to get rid of my animals or move out of the inn."

"Did anybody ever show you the letter your mother left?" he asked hesitantly.

She nodded. "Father McCarren gave it to me when I was eighteen." She traced a pattern on Tidbit's back. "It just said she couldn't take care of me anymore and she was trusting that God's servants would. That was all."

His heart filled with pain for her. "Do you remember anything about her?"

"Not much. A smile, a smell. Being cold at night. Her name was Bridget Larkin."

"Did you ever try to find her?" Maybe this was something he could do for her. "I could—"

"I doubt it, Eli. Father McCarren couldn't find her, and she's been gone almost twenty years."

"But—"

"No." The tone was final, resolved.

"Was there a father listed on your birth certificate?"

"Michael Jones. No occupation, address or birthplace listed. Could be anybody."

"So she left you without even a past," he said quietly.

"Yes," she agreed. "My life pretty much started the day she abandoned me."

He looked at the numerous animals sprawled around the living room. She had adopted every one of them. They were her family now, in place of the human one she didn't have. "I guess now I understand why you feel so strongly about abandonment."

"*Everyone* should feel strongly about it. Do you have any idea how many kids are abandoned each year as if they were just so much disposable garbage? Often by people who go on to have *more* children. Or how many animals get dumped by the roadside or in the woods?'' Her voice was fierce and rough. "At least I grew up and learned to rationalize what my mother did. But my dogs will never be capable of understanding why they were abandoned. And because of that, they're always afraid *I'll* leave them, too. They save their food, they cry when they're punished, they panic when they get lost in the woods or when I go away for more than a day.''

He groped for her hand and held it in a painful grip. "I wasn't trying to make light of your adopting all of them,'' he assured her. "I believe you.''

She lowered her eyes and slumped against him. "I'm sorry,'' she mumbled.

"Don't apologize.'' He nuzzled her hair and drew her firmly against him. "I won't say don't *ever* apologize, because sometimes you're a maddening woman, but don't apologize for telling me how you feel.''

"Okay,'' she whispered against his shoulder.

He felt the quiver of her slender shoulders beneath his hands, the fierce hunger in her soul when she answered his kiss, and her eager willingness as he scooped her up and carried her into the bedroom. He laid her gently across her four-poster bed and walked back to the door.

"Out!'' he snapped at Tidbit and three others who had joined Fiona on the bed. After some further insistence, they finally departed, and he closed the door firmly behind them.

"There are some things I just don't want to share with the crowd,'' Eli said as he joined Fiona on the bed.

He undressed her slowly, one garment at a time, exploring and enjoying each aspect of her lovely, delicate body as it was revealed to him in the moonlight pouring through the windows. No woman had ever made him feel so greedy and generous at once, no one had ever inspired such a combination of savage excitement and tender affection in him.

He wanted tonight to be like his sweetest fantasies, like her earthiest dreams. When they were both naked, he held her so she sat with her back pressed against his chest, her body imprisoned between his muscular legs.

He smoothed his palms up and down her arms in light, circular motions. Fiona tilted her head back, and her chestnut hair spilled across his shoulder, teasing him with its feathery softness. He ran his hand up the smooth column of her throat and lowered his head to taste the creamy skin of her shoulder.

Fiona sighed when she felt the tender heat of his open mouth on her shoulder, her neck, her cheek. His stroking, soothing hands made her feel cherished and valuable. The hard wall of his chest behind her made him seem vast and all-powerful. The dark blond hair of his chest tickled her back, just as the darker hair of his groin tickled her soft bottom.

He whispered into her ear, setting her on fire, setting her free, promising her they would do anything she wanted, anything to make her explode with pleasure.

"Tell me a secret," he whispered.

"I stared at your...jeans a lot when you first came here," she admitted on a whisper. She felt him smile against her hair.

"Really?" He sounded pleased. "What were you thinking?"

"You know what I was thinking. Your turn."

"Let's see..." he said consideringly. "How about this? I can be unreasonably stubborn when I don't get my way."

"That's hardly a secret. Try harder," she said, laughing at him.

He rubbed against her. "Hard enough?"

Fiona's breasts rose and fell with rapid, shallow breaths. "A secret," she said in a strangled voice.

"Okay, a secret," he said. He brushed her nipples with his fingertips. "Tough guy that I am—"

"Humph."

"Pink is my favorite color." He pinched them. "Just this shade of pink."

She dug her nails into his thighs. "I'm so glad."

He got more creative in his playing and teasing. "Do you like it when I touch you like that?"

She made a high-pitched sound and nodded emphatically.

"Where else do you want me to touch you?" he asked knowingly. When she was silent he coaxed, "Don't go all shy on me, sweetheart. You've already admitted that you stared at my—"

"Here," she said roughly, guiding his hand. "Touch me here."

"Like this?" he whispered.

"Yes." She sighed and started to move her hips in a slow, instinctual rhythm. "Just like that. Yes, yes, yes... Ohhhh."

He was breathing raggedly. "Know where I want you to touch me?"

She didn't even bother to answer him, but shifted and fumbled and found what she sought. He tightened his arm around her and started mumbling incoherently against her hair, encouraging her, begging her, promising her. And despite his obvious absorption in what she was doing to him, he kept her on the fine edge of pleasure with tender, commanding hands. Someday she would ask him how he knew so much about a woman's body. But this definitely wasn't the moment, she thought, as pleasure seared her senses.

He gripped her waist with strong hands and gently eased her forward until her face rested against the mound of crumpled quilt before them. She clutched at the soft fabric and braced her elbows against the mattress, moaning throatily as she felt his warm palm slide down her spine, over her bottom, and between her legs to stroke her again, to tease her one last time before he entered her body with a long, slow thrust.

She began to move with him in a primitive rhythm of unbearable intensity. With his chest pressed against her back, she could feel the thundering of his heart as he slid against her. His seeking mouth caressed her shoulders and neck and hair, his harsh breath roared through her ears with his rapturous whispers, and his muscular arms, braced on either side of her, trembled beneath his weight as he surged into her.

Fulfillment flowed through her with sudden, scalding heat, and she cried out as her body went liquid and weak beneath him, pliantly welcoming his own climax. Sighing softly, they fumbled to clasp hands before nestling into the covers together to rest after the explosion of their passion.

The night was wild and peaceful by turns, as they gave free reign to their fantasies and slaked their passion, then rested languidly in each other's arms, only to begin anew as a look or touch stirred desire within them again. Eli worshiped the dark mystery of her woman's body. He reveled in the fulfilling sound of her sighs and moans. Fiona explored him with endless delight and fascination, marveling at how uniquely beautiful he was in the moon-streaked night.

When they weren't loving, they were talking, whispering to each other on the pillows without caution or concern, sharing all their thoughts and questions.

Eli forgot about everything and everyone but her. She became the whole world to him and her bed became the entire universe. The answer to every question or longing he'd ever known was here, in the warmth of her arms, in the tight sheath of her body, in the secret longing of her whispers, and he boldly sought what he wanted.

He was delirious with pleasure and incoherent with exhaustion by the time his body demanded rest. He was too tired to even ask her if she, too, had found this to be the most glorious night of her life. But the way she clung to him, even in her sleep, made him believe that perhaps it was the same for her. Perhaps she also knew that together they could have everything a man and woman needed from each other.

He floated to sleep believing that everything would be all right from now on.

Nine

"**H**ow can you be so dense?" Fiona snapped at Eli as she paced up and down the length of the staff room. "I'm telling you, someone was here last night!"

"That's pure speculation," he snapped back. "Unfounded and, I might add, hysterical."

"I am not hysterical!"

"Then why are you shouting?" he shouted.

"Will you guys please shut *up* for a second?" Brian pleaded.

Fiona turned to Brian and made a suggestion that shocked both men into momentary silence.

"She's pretty uptight, Eli," Brian finally said with an air of authority. "I've never heard her use language like that before."

"She's not the only one," Eli grumbled.

It had been a perfect morning. He and Fiona had awoken in each other's arms and made love lazily in the borning light of the new day. Then they quietly had coffee together in her cozy kitchen and walked to the kennel in a silence so perfectly harmonious that he had known there was no need to talk yet about what was happening between them, what was happening in his heart. Everything had seemed as clear as crystal, as simple as breathing. Yes, it had been a perfect morning.

Until now, that is. *Now* he wanted to shake her until her teeth rattled.

Houdini was missing. Brian and Eli came to the obvious conclusion that the dog had once again escaped. Fiona insisted he had been dognapped by their elusive prowler.

"Fi-ona," Eli said, forcibly pushing her into a chair. "I'm not saying it's impossible that your prowler took him, just that it's unlikely. Houdini has escaped four times in the past without help. Until yesterday, I would have said it was impossible for a dog to leave a building by way of the chimney. He's a pretty amazing animal," Eli added grudgingly.

"I'm telling you, I *know* it's different this time."

"How do you know?" he asked reasonably.

She looked at him in mute fury.

Eli sighed. "Fiona, woman's intuition is not evidence."

"What is?" she challenged.

"Footprints," he said. "With all this fresh snow on the ground—"

"I doubt that," said Brian. "We've been open for an hour. By my count, nearly thirty people have already come and gone. If only I'd realized he was missing earlier."

"If only you'd arrived on time, you mean," Fiona fumed.

"Give him a break, Fiona, there's still twelve inches of snow out there," Eli chided.

"How dare you interfere between me and my staff!" she snapped. She took a deep, angry breath and announced that *she* was going outside to look for footprints, and what her hotshot international security expert did was his own damn business.

Eli gave a martyred sigh and followed her outside. Unfortunately, Brian's estimation proved to be right. With a dozen staff members and thirty customers tromping around the environs, it was impossible to discover one set of footprints in the snow that didn't belong. Fiona railed at Eli that surely this was supposed to be his job, to figure out this kind of thing. With a patience foreign to his nature, he ignored her.

When it became clear that nothing could be proved, Fiona stormed back inside the kennel and took all the measures she usually took when Houdini ran away. Eli had some nerve to sleep in her bed, listen to her secrets and then doubt her expert opinion about one of her own boarders disappearing. The more he tried to be reasonable—pointing out that all the evidence in Houdini's run supported his theory as much as it supported hers, double-checking all the possible means of entry to the kennel to satisfy her—the more incensed Fiona became.

The local animal warden returned Houdini that afternoon. Although Fiona was relieved to have him back, his return didn't improve the situation between herself and Eli.

"Where was he found?" Eli asked, following her into the kitchen.

"About three miles from here," she mumbled.

"Which, I am professionally bound to point out, is about how far he would have gotten by himself."

"Or he could have escaped from his captor," Fiona countered.

"Why would your prowler take a mutt like Houdini?" Eli challenged.

"Stop calling him *my* prowler as if he were a figment of my imagination!" Her eyes glinted greenly as she narrowed them suddenly. "Or is that what you really think?"

"No." He shifted. "Not really."

"What does that mean?"

"It means something funny was going on here. But nothing odd has happened since my first night here." He considered the events of recent days and added, "I mean, nothing that seems suspicious."

"That's it!" Fiona snapped her fingers. "You weren't here last night. That's why he came back!"

"Fiona—"

She gasped. "That means he's watching us," she whispered. She looked around the room as if it might be bugged.

"It doesn't make sense," Eli said in frustration. "If someone is desperate enough to watch the kennel for days on end, he's also desperate—or unbalanced—enough to do some kind of damage. To steal or vandalize. To attack someone."

"Now, look, Eli. *I* read Ed McBain. I know that motive is about the last thing you can count on to make sense."

"I'm not talking about motive. Even if we disregard *why* he comes, we can't figure out *what* he does when he comes here. Except for the incident with the computer being accessed, there's not even any reasonable evidence that he *has* been here." Eli lost himself in the confusion of his final statement and sank into a chair. "I have a headache."

Fiona looked at his golden head as he lowered it and raked his fingers through his eternally tumbled hair. Everything inside of her hurt, had been hurting since this morning. He just didn't want to be here, and he couldn't have made it clearer. He still thought this whole affair was a waste of his time, and he wanted to leave. It didn't matter that she had given herself to him heart and soul all through the night, he wanted to go now.

"Well, why don't you just get out of here, then?" she said in a rough voice. Pride lifted her chin. "If you think it's all just a wild-goose chase and you're not even going to treat me like an adult, then just go."

Eli reached for Fiona and missed as she whirled to leave. "Hey!" he called after her, but she ignored him and practically ran out of the room. He stared after her in confusion. What the hell was that all about?

He replayed their conversation in his mind and scowled. So they didn't agree about this. So what? Did that made it all right for her to simply throw him out after everything they had shared during the past couple of days? Eli ground his teeth together. She was a maddening woman! But he wasn't leaving, and he damn well wasn't going to let her throw him out. This was no longer just professional. Now it was personal, for better or worse.

With renewed determination to come out a winner in this nutty place and among these lunatic people, he stomped into the back of the kennel to get Bundle. At least the damn dog appreciated him. At least the dog didn't turn around and snarl at him as soon as he got a little close to it.

"At least the *dog*," he told an astonished Nadine as he stalked past her, "is a little bit reasonable!"

He spent the rest of the day continuing to check up on the various people who had threatened Oak Hill with mayhem, violence, or lawsuits during the past few months. Fiona only spoke to him once all day, and that was to ask him to handle Mr. Snyder again.

"He's back?" Eli asked Fiona incredulously as he tossed a dog biscuit to Bundle.

"Yes," she said in a low voice. "He's raising hell in the lobby right now. Something has really lit a fire under him, Eli. He's hysterical."

"You mean as opposed to his calm, reasonable behavior during his last visit?" Eli said dryly.

"He's scaring me," Fiona admitted.

"Of course I'll handle him, sweetheart." Eli pushed his paperwork away and rose from the table in the staff room. He hesitated for a moment and said, "Uh, are his kids with him?"

"No."

"Not that I was worried or anything."

"Of course not." Fiona said no more. She knew his masculine ego was bruised enough already.

"Stay," he said to Bundle.

Bundle followed him to the door and whined when Eli closed it firmly in his face. The scene in the lobby was as bad as Fiona had indicated.

"I'll sue you for every penny you've got! I'll turn your name to mud! I'll get you for this! I demand you give me my little Rocky!" Mr. Snyder was screaming into Brian's face. Brian stared at him in helpless amazement.

"Call the cops," Eli said immediately.

"Can't you handle him?" Fiona said worriedly.

Eli looked insulted. "Of course I can handle him. But people usually come to their senses when you call the police."

Fiona left Eli to deal with Mr. Snyder and went into the office to phone the police. While she explained her problem to them, she wished for the first time that Vicky hadn't shown so much faith in her by leaving her to run things alone during the holidays. Was this pressure never going to let up?

However, as Eli had predicted, the knowledge that the police were on their way had a somewhat tranquilizing effect on Mr. Snyder. Only somewhat. He muttered more dire threats and slander, but at least he left willingly. Eli's main difficulty was in preventing him from damaging the lobby furniture before he left. After all the indignities he had suffered, Eli felt relieved to confirm he still had all his skills intact. Even with his injuries, he was able to throw Mr. Snyder—a fifth dan black belt—to the floor with relative ease. He secretly hoped Fiona had noticed.

But when he entered the office to see Fiona, she already had other matters on her mind.

"Have you called Mrs. Snyder about all this?" Brian demanded.

Fiona frowned. "Yes. I don't know what to do. The number turned out to be a resort hotel in Hawaii. I said I was calling from Oak Hill Pet Motel to talk to her about Rocky. The hotel said she's refusing to answer all calls. What's more," Fiona added in perplexity, "they said if we keep harassing her, the hotel will report us to the police."

"What do you suppose that means?" Brian said. He looked at Eli with sudden interest. "Hey, Snyder must be harassing her, too. Eli, do you think there could be a connection?"

"With the problems here?" Eli asked. He shook his head. "I don't see how. Your troubles started before Rocky ever arrived. And Mr. Snyder may be the most colorful of your customers, but he's not the only one who's threatened Fiona this week." He smiled wryly. "Don't you just love the holiday spirit?"

"If only there were a pattern, an M.O., some kind of clear reason for these disturbances," Brian said with open frustration.

"You're starting to sound like Eli," Fiona said. It was clearly not a compliment. She left the room without another glance at either of them. They looked at each other and shrugged.

It was after the office had closed for business and the kids were finishing up their evening chores at the back of the kennel that Eli finally approached Fiona. Hopefully she had cooled down a little by now. He and Bundle found her folding piles of blankets and towels in the laundry room.

"Haven't you had enough for one day?" he said gently to her. "Let one of the kids do that."

She shrugged wearily. "It needs to be done."

She was avoiding his eyes. He frowned distractedly at the dog when it walked under his feet. "Sit," he ordered. Bundle sneezed and looked blank. "Good dog," Eli said resignedly.

"Training's going well, I see."

"Any advice?"

"Sure." She put down the rug she was folding. She grabbed a firm hold of Bundle's collar with one hand and placed the other hand on his rump. She pulled up on his neck, pressed down on his rump, and said, "Sit!"

Bundle sat. Fiona praised him.

"Hey, that's great!" Eli said.

"Now just do that a hundred times a day for a few days, and he'll figure it out." She went back to her laundry and added, "Of course, there's no point in teaching him manners if you're just going to leave him behind when you go."

Eli frowned, not liking the careful neutrality of her tone which managed to sound so condemning. "*I* didn't abandon him, Fiona," he pointed out.

"I know. But the more time he spends with you, the harder it will be on him when you leave. It will be just like being abandoned all over again."

There was a long, heavy silence. Eli stared at her, realizing there was more going on between them than a discussion about whether or not he adopted the dog. "Fiona . . ."

"I think you'd better sleep here tonight, don't you?" she said quickly.

"Yes. It was careless of me to stay at your house all night." He smiled and touched her cheek. "You make me half-witted when you touch me."

She didn't shrink from his touch. But she went as still as a frightened deer. Whatever was going on, Eli intended to take advantage of the ground he had gained with her last night.

"Stay here with me," he said huskily.

Fiona shook her head mutely and paid intense attention to the towel she was folding.

Eli moved closer to her. He placed his hands around her waist and pulled her firmly against the length of his body. "I want you," he whispered. "Look at me."

"Let me go." Her voice was barely audible.

Eli heard the fear in her voice, but when he smoothed his palm across her breast he felt the way her body tightened with excitement. There was a tug of war inside her, and he didn't think it was because she had developed a sudden aversion to sex.

"Stay with me and we'll talk," he coaxed. "We don't have to do anything else unless you decide you want to."

Fiona's breath started coming fast. Her heart pounded painfully. If she stayed, she knew she'd want to do a lot more than talk. And what would they talk about anyhow? The terror of having her heart ripped out of her chest again? The guilt and humiliation of wanting and waiting for someone who would never come back, no matter what promises had been made?

She backed away from him, into a corner. "Leave me alone," she said. "I mean..."

"What do you mean?" He tried to keep his voice gentle.

She groped for something to say. "Look, today made it clear that we've just overstepped our bounds. It's better if we don't..." She closed her eyes, fighting for control.

"No, it's not." He reached for her.

"Don't!" She pushed against his chest and slipped past him.

"Fiona, just talk to me," he pleaded.

"I'm going home!"

He could hear the tears in her voice. The last thing in the world he wanted was to make her cry, so he let her go. He felt distinctly depressed as he helped the kids lock up the kennel, double-checked everything, then made up his humble bed in the lounge. Bundle watched him with liquid brown eyes, and Eli's own sense of desolation made him decide to keep the dog with him instead of putting him back in his run for the night.

Since he had finished his spy novel, he decided to turn on the black-and-white portable TV that Fiona kept stowed away in one of the closets.

"Well, what's it to be, Bundle? *Nightline* or a rerun of *Magnum, P.I.*?"

Eli stared unseeingly at the television screen for almost an hour, mulling things over. Fiona had been abandoned as a child. Abandoned by her mother, by the one person a kid trusted most. And since then, she hadn't taken on anyone permanent in her life.

When Eli thought about it, he realized that in the whole time he had been here, and in all the pillow talk they had shared, she had never mentioned another person who was at the core of her life.

He had learned that she wrote only occasionally and perfunctorily to the nun who had tried to mother her. She seldom saw or spoke to the one girl who had been like a sister to her at the orphanage. Somewhere in the night he had asked her about men, wondering who had been crazy enough to let her go. There had been a few, but only one that had counted particularly.

"Why did it end?" he had asked, touching her satiny skin, drowning in her subtle scent.

She had shrugged sleepily. "He had a problem with commitment."

And after her youth, Eli realized, Fiona couldn't handle anyone who had a problem with commitment. He suspected Fiona herself had a problem with commitment. So she filled her house with dogs and cats and one sociopathic bird, all of whom were abandoned waifs, none of whom would ever leave her.

"Well, listen, Bundle," Eli said to the drooling dog, "I *don't* have a problem with commitment."

Bundle's ears pricked.

"Okay, you're wondering why I'm not married at thirty-four. That's easy. I've never been in love before." He stopped and his eyes widened. "That's really it, isn't it? I'm in love with her." He glared at the dog, who had risen to his feet. "Well, don't look so surprised, you must have seen it coming. I stopped being girl-crazy when I was in my twenties. Why else would I think about Fiona day and night, lose sleep over her, act like a bumbling amateur every time I think she's in trouble? Why else would I still be hanging around this crazy place, if I weren't out of my mind over the woman?''

Bundle tilted his head. "Do you think it's permanent?" Eli took a breath and straightened his shoulders. "It *feels* pretty permanent. It feels like she's sunk all the way into my bones." Bundle made a noise in his throat. "Oh, I agree, she's a lot to take on. Unpredictable, demanding, temperamental, and *all* those dogs—no offense intended, Bundle. But..." Eli smiled foolishly. "But she's got some great qualities, don't you think?" He frowned. "Hell, what am I asking a dog for? I'm getting to be as crazy as she is."

He shook his head wryly and then realized that the dog was indeed listening—but not to him. Bundle's whole body was poised tensely, his eyes focused on some distant point and his ears pricked to catch any slight sound.

Eli heard nothing definite, but he could tell the moment Bundle did. The dog slunk forward, looked at Eli, and crouched. After one more glance at Eli, Bundle made a sound somewhere between a moan and a growl.

"My God, it's him," Eli muttered. "At last." For the first time since his arrival at Oak Hill, he reached into his overnight bag and pulled out his gun.

He checked it, then said to Bundle, "Stay." Bundle tried to follow him out of the room. "Dammit, we should have learned this word by now, Bundle. Stay, *stay*. No. Stay." Bundle's brown eyes begged not to be left alone in this dark, scary place, but Eli was adamant. "Go on. *Letterman*'s almost on. You'll like him, really. Go. Stay. You know what I mean."

After he had finally convinced the dog to stay behind, Eli stealthily crept into the vast, dark, back halls of the kennel, where mournful howls floated on the air. Where the man who tormented Fiona's nights lay in wait for him.

A moment later, there was no need for stealth. A moment later, he heard a woman scream, and he knew it was Fiona.

Instinct guided him to the nearest light switch. He called her name but got no answer. His heart pounded so frantically it hurt. He ran through the back halls, checking every room and door.

"Fiona!" he called. "Fi— Oh, my God!"

He found her near the side entrance. The door was open, letting in the cold night air.

Fiona lay facedown on the floor, unconscious.

Ten

――――

"**I**'m all right. Will you stop hovering over me!" Fiona said irritably.

"You're not supposed to get out of bed. Doctor's orders," Brian said.

"Where's Eli?" Fiona asked plaintively, wanting him. He hadn't left her side since she had woken up in the emergency room the previous night to find him holding her hand and begging her to be all right. He had taken her home, handled the police, fed her dogs and watched over her all day. He had been lover, friend and parent to her.

But now it was dark out and she had awoken to find Brian hovering over her. "I want Eli," she said crossly.

"He's doing his job," Brian said.

"What?"

"He's standing guard at the kennel. It's nearly midnight." He sat in a chair on the far side of the bedroom and said eagerly, "So, tell me how you got conked on the head."

"Didn't Eli tell you?"

"No," Brian said gravely. "He just told me that you belong to him and that it's bad enough that I gave you a sexy negligee, but if I so much as touch you tonight, he'll kill me."

"Really?" Fiona said interestedly.

"I tried to take it in stride. He was pretty uptight."

"I see." She tried to settle into a more comfortable position and winced as her concussed skull throbbed.

"So what happened?" Brian asked with ghoulish curiosity.

"I walked over to the kennel about midnight."

"Why?" he asked, looking perplexed. Then a disgustingly sly look entered his blue eyes. "*Ohhh*, of course."

She glared at him, but she could hardly deny it. After tossing and turning for over an hour the previous night, she had decided that she was acting like a child. For the last time, though. She wanted to make love, and wanted to talk. Despite what she had told Eli the previous night about her only serious past relationship, she suspected that *she* was the one with a commitment problem. If you committed yourself to someone, then he could hurt you.

He could leave you.

"Come on, what happened next?" Brian prodded.

"I unlocked the side door and walked in. I felt creepy, like I was being watched or followed. I had only walked about ten feet inside the door when I decided I'd feel better if I turned on the light. So I turned around to go back to the light switch by the door and..." She permitted herself a little dramatic pause. "And there was someone standing there. I screamed, and he hit me over the head with something. I think it was a flashlight."

"You're sure it was a man?" Brian asked.

"He was too tall and wide to be a woman."

"Did you see what he looked like?"

"Barely," she said. "It was so dark. He was white, male, clean-shaven. That's it. Not remotely familiar."

"And then Eli turned on the lights and shouted your name, and the guy split," Brian surmised.

"I guess so." She frowned. "Maybe the prowler's not watching us after all, or he would have known Eli was there."

"Maybe he knew Eli was there," Brian countered, "but he's so desperate for whatever he's after that he decided to risk it."

Their eyes met.

"Surely no one could be stupid enough . . ." Fiona began.

"Of course, Eli's trying to make it look like he's *not* there tonight," Brian said, his smooth forehead creasing in sudden worry.

Fiona started to push herself up on her elbows. "Whatever he wants, this guy must be very unstable. Or irretrievably stupid. And Eli's there alone."

Brian ran a hand through his blond mop. "But this is Eli's job. He'll know how to handle it." He didn't sound so certain.

"Maybe under normal circumstances," Fiona argued, "but he's still got a nasty gash on his head, his right arm is practically useless, he's trying to hide the fact that he's still limping slightly and he hasn't had a full night's sleep in days and days."

"Where do you think you're going?" Brian asked as Fiona started to slide out of bed.

"I've got to help him." She winced as she sat up and her head started throbbing as if it would burst.

"Fiona, he'll kill me if I let you out of here tonight," Brian said pleadingly.

"I'll die if anything happens to him while I'm lying around here."

He paused and looked at her seriously. "You've got it that bad?"

Her eyes met his with open honesty. "Oh, Brian, it's just awful."

"That's not what the Romantic poets say."

"You flunked that course," Fiona reminded him crisply. "Anyhow, what do they know? Now help me get dressed."

"No, Fifi, he really *would* kill me for that."

"This is no time to be squeamish."

With some effort and considerable pain, they managed to work Fiona's body into enough warm clothing to go out into the frigid night. There was a suspicious moment when she could have sworn Brian was blushing, but she was too concerned about Eli to care.

No one in her life had ever coddled and cuddled and cared for her the way Eli had for the past twenty-four hours. He jumped out of his chair every time she drew a deep breath, he hovered over her with the desire to provide for her every need, he nurtured her in a thousand small ways. She could sense his presence even as she slept, and she had felt bereft to wake and find him gone and Brian filling his chair. And now he was alone in the dark, waiting for the fiend that had knocked her out last night.

Their past differences of opinion didn't matter anymore. When push came to shove, Eli Becker came through for her as no one else ever had. And it wasn't guilt, either. She knew that.

She smiled with all the fond affection of love. No, when Eli felt guilty, he fidgeted and got cranky. Or else he got amorous. And she could handle him either way.

"Ready?" she said to Brian.

"Let's go. Better hold on to me."

Fiona slipped her arm through his, realizing for the first time just how close Brian was to being a man. He was already bigger than Eli. His heart was in the right place. Now if only the rest of him would shape up.

They walked through the snow-laden oak grove in silence. Fiona had to concentrate all her strength on each step, trying not to fall into a weary heap, trying to ignore the shards of pain splintering her skull. There was a bad moment when she thought she might be sick, but she ignored that, too. She was propelled by the urgency of her instincts. She had to get to Eli.

"Oh, my God," Brian whispered tensely as they came out of the grove. He crouched down. "Look!"

Clinging to him for support, Fiona searched the darkness. She drew in a sharp, terrified breath when she saw him. The dark, bulky figure of her nightmares paused a moment in the moon-brilliant night, and then slipped around the side of the kennel building.

"He's got to be crazy," Brian murmured. "It's almost as bright as day out here."

"But it's pitch-dark in there," Fiona said fearfully. She could see even from here that Eli had turned out all of the lights in order to encourage the intruder. Not even the usual safety lights remained. "Come on." Her voice carried an intense determination born of the desire to help the man she loved.

Eli stalked silently around the darkened halls of the kennel, treading lightly so as not to wake any of the boarders. Every instinct told him that the prowler would return tonight, as crazy as that would be. And Eli was waiting for him.

Now it was personal. Now the guy had attacked Eli's woman, and Eli would make him pay for that.

He checked the office. No one around. Fiona's mittens lay on a file cabinet. He picked them up and squeezed them for a minute, as tightly as he had squeezed her hand during the most awful night of his life. When he had found her lying there on the floor, cold as ice and white as a ghost, he thought he would die on the spot. Only the knowledge that he had to help her had kept him going. Only the awareness that she needed him to keep his head had kept him from losing it.

He wondered if she would ever forgive him for doubting the seriousness of this case. He would spend the rest of his life making it up to her. It had only taken a few hours of terror, and a few more hours of caring for her and thanking God she was safe, for him to realize that a lifetime was what he wanted from her.

He left the office and stalked down the front hallway. The store was empty and peaceful. So was the lounge.

They would make a good life together; they were a natural combination. He was a protector; she was a nurturer. He was a provider; she was a nest-maker. He was volatile; she was determined. He had a predator's instinct; she had a woman's intuition.

They could get through anything together. He hadn't know how much he had needed her, how desperately he was looking for her, until he actually met and fell in love with her.

He checked the kitchen and the staff room. His nerves quivered, sensing the edge of danger, but there was no one there. He paused thoughtfully for a minute, then continued his soft-footed rounds in the back of the kennel.

As soon as this business was settled, he'd have it out with her. True, they hadn't known each other long, but they knew each other well. When it was right, a man didn't need months to decide. Eli was more certain of Fiona than he had ever been of anything in his life, and he wasn't a man who made mistakes with the big decisions. Only the little things, he thought derisively, as his right knee pained him again. Maybe he shouldn't have been so stubborn about having it examined.

The days would be filled with love and laughter, fighting and making up, work and play, children and stray dogs and unwanted birds. And the nights would be full of enchantment and ecstasy—the rich feast of love. Ah, yes, the nights...

He was checking the wings when he became aware of it. The sound was so inconsequential that he would have dismissed it if his senses weren't so sharply tuned to the slightest nuance of danger. He couldn't identify the exact source of the noise, but he knew it came from somewhere near the feed room. He knew his prey was nearby. With a quick breath of exultation, Eli crouched and crept closer to his quarry.

Within moments, instinct guided him to the maze where they kept bags of dry dog food in ceiling-high stacks, shelves of canned dog food, cat food and stores of cleaning supplies. It was pitch-black here, but his senses focused on the intruder.

He was here. Eli could feel him, smell him, hear him. In his mind's eye, he could see him. In another moment the man would creep clear of the protective barrier of stacked shelves, and Eli would take him.

His whole body tensed the instant he became aware of another presence. Another person? Had the guy brought help? Eli immediately shifted his original plan, now quickly working out how to take both of them at once.

Then he sensed the tension coming from his initial target. The intruders hadn't come together, Eli realized with astonishment.

Good Lord! Just how the hell many people were breaking into Oak Hill at night? He really would have to speak to Fiona about this, he decided irritably.

The second intruder was hesitant. And noisy. Eli shook his head, feeling the professional's natural contempt for such amateurism. He heard some whispering and realized that there were two of them. *Well, hell, why don't we just open a six-pack and all get acquainted?*

A moment later the original intruder made a flurry of movement, noticeable for its clumsiness. Didn't anybody know how to move with stealth anymore? Eli wondered critically. There was some grappling and grunting. Eli lowered the muzzle of his gun and considered letting them all just beat each other's brains out.

Then he heard a feminine gasp. He nearly keeled over with shock. He recognized even the sound of her breath, so her voice a moment later merely served as confirmation of what he already knew.

"The light won't work!" Fiona exclaimed.

Eli had turned off the main switch. Having paced off the length and breadth of the kennel, and having memorized where every obstacle was, he figured he would have the advantage in the dark. Of course, he hadn't counted on that *maddening*—not to mention injured—woman crawling out of bed and coming here in the middle of the night.

There was another gasp. It came from Brian who, Eli reflected furiously, had better make his peace with God. *I'll kill you for letting her walk right into the middle of this.*

"Fiona," Brian choked out, "he's got a gun."

"How do you know?" she asked frantically.

"It's digging into my stomach."

Fiona gasped again. Then anger took over. "A gun? You brought a *gun* in here, you scumbucket?"

"Please," Brian pleaded weakly, "don't antagonize the man."

"How could you bring a loaded weapon into a kennelful of animals, you filthy, rotten, slimy—"

"Shut up!" said the prowler in an aggrieved tone.

Eli stilled the panic rising inside him. A gun. The guy had a gun. He could hurt Fiona a lot worse than he already had. *Think,* he ordered himself. *You can't help her if you lose your cool.*

A small glow of illumination made Eli pull back onto the shadows a moment later. The prowler was holding a pocket lighter in one hand and pointing his weapon at Brian and Fiona with the other.

"Where's Rocky?" he demanded.

"What?" Brian said incredulously.

"The Snyder dog, dammit! Where is he?"

Fiona stared at the man for a moment. "This is not an appropriate time to visit a boarder," she said at last.

Eli didn't know whether he wanted to laugh or throttle her. She shouldn't get sassy with a man pointing a gun at her. Eli noticed then, as Fiona probably had, that the guy's hand was shaking. He wasn't a cold-blooded killer; that much seemed apparent. The problem was, as nervous and as jumpy as the man seemed to be, Eli couldn't confront him while Fiona and Brian were exposed.

He would have to distract the stranger and give Brian and Fiona time to take cover. One obvious, immediate solution presented itself. Dread overwhelmed him. If the situation were any less dire, he would have searched for another possibility. But he'd lose control of himself if he had to spend another moment watching Fiona talk to the barrel of a gun. He turned and moved with silent speed, making his way to the wings of dog runs.

Fiona held her body rigid and wondered where Eli was. She and Brian had found the edge of the side door splintered by forced entry. The prowler had finally become desperate enough to leave evidence of his trespass. But now that Fiona had proof, she wasn't in a position to relish it. She and Brian were looking down the barrel of a gun, and there was no sign of Eli. She wondered if this man had somehow already managed to shoot him. The stranger's next question relieved her, but only for a moment.

"Where's your private dick?" he demanded.

"I beg your pardon?" she said icily.

"Your shamus, your flatfoot, your snoop."

"Good question," Brian muttered.

"First you want Rocky, now you want a snoop. Are you sure you're in the right place?" Where *was* Eli? Should she be stalling like this, or should she inspire Brian to tackle the man? Handing over Rocky was obviously out of the question. She couldn't simply give one of her boarders to some lunatic with a gun.

Their attention was diverted by a sudden burst of barking from the kennel wings. Fiona's heart jumped. That must be where Eli was! What the devil was he doing?

"What's going on here?" the stranger demanded nervously. His gun started wavering.

Fiona heard heavy breath and the slap of big paws behind her. It was chillingly familiar. Brian's body whipped around next to her. The stranger's eyes widened and a moment later the lighter went out. Out of the pitch blackness, Fiona heard Brian cry, "Oh, my God! Who let Myron out?"

"Arrrgh!" the stranger screamed. Myron barked. The gun went off.

"Fiona! Are you all right? Fiona!" Through the ringing in her ears, Fiona heard Eli's voice, loud and frantic.

"Yes!" She called. Then worriedly, "Myron! Myron! If you've hurt Myron, you slug, I—ooof! Myron!" she cried joyfully as one big paw punched her in the stomach and a soft tongue washed her face.

"Did it ever occur to either of you that it might have been *me* he shot?" came Brian's outraged voice.

Fiona's attention, however, was completely absorbed by the sounds of a fight only a few feet away from her. She could hear thumps, thuds, grunts and groans. A moment later Eli and the prowler crashed into one of the shelves of canned dog food. The entire thing came tumbling down. Myron clearly thought it was all terribly exciting, and he left Fiona to go join in the fray. A minute later she heard Eli's pained, furious voice.

"No! Bad dog! No!" Then Myron barked again. There were some scrambling sounds. "Dammit! Get off me, you smelly beast!"

Fiona crawled toward the two of them, dragging Brian with her. "Myron! Off!" she snapped as she and Brian tugged at the dog's collar.

Eli drew in a few gulps of air once Myron was removed from his chest. Through gritted teeth he said, "I'm never doing this again!"

"He's gone!" Brian exclaimed suddenly.

"He got away while I was pinned down by your friend here," Eli said in injured tones. "And I've dropped my gun."

"You have a gun? You brought a *gun* in here?" Fiona said furiously.

"Not now, Fiona." Eli's tone silenced her. "Brian, go to the fuse box, switch all the lights back on. And you," he added sternly to Fiona, "stay here."

He and Brian dashed off, leaving Fiona sitting in a heap of dog food while Myron drooled on her. "Of all the nerve," she said. "I'm the boss here."

A moment later all the lights came on, hurting her eyes with their brilliance after the long, agonizing moments in the dark. She heard a shout and a thud, and she surmised that Eli had once again found their prowler. The sounds were coming from near the wings.

She didn't care what he had said. She couldn't just sit there while he went alone after an armed and dangerous criminal. She hopped up and, followed by Myron, trotted into the back hallway.

One glance at the furious fight told her all she needed to know. Eli was too fast and agile to be damaged much by the other man, but the stranger outweighed him by about sixty pounds. What's more, the deep cut on Eli's forehead had opened again, his sprained and mangled right hand was clearly useless to him and his limp was worse. She gnawed on her lower lip worriedly, wondering how to help.

"I've got it!" Brian said from behind her. "Fifi, take it!"

She whirled to find Brian hauling a high-pressure hose in from a kennel wing. "A hose?" she said blankly. She took it from Brian just an instant before Myron knocked him gleefully to the ground.

When she turned back to the fight, the stranger kicked Eli in his bad knee. Eli fell, and the stranger had time to crawl under a grooming crate to grope for his gun.

Without thinking, Fiona turned the hose on the stranger. In this weather, the water was cold enough to freeze a polar bear. The man howled as if he was being tortured and starting crawling in the opposite direction. Eli came to his feet and shouted at Fiona to turn the water off. When she did, he jumped on top of the man and delivered three impressive left-handed blows.

The man lay limp and docile at last. Eli whipped off his belt and tied the man's hands behind his back. Then he rose stiffly to his feet and turned to Fiona. He walked unsteadily toward her, a conquering hero, a proud warrior, a knight in shining armor coming to collect his reward. Fiona's heart pounded wildly in her chest at the fiery look of pure sexuality blazing in those golden-brown eyes.

Then he slipped in the icy water spreading across the floor. He flew through the air in a graceless arc and landed on his head.

"Eli!" Fiona cried. She slid across the floor and knelt next to him in an inch of cold water. "Oh, my God! Brian, come here!"

Brian crawled to the door and slammed it in Myron's face, locking him in the aisle of one of the wings. Then he skidded over to Fiona and tried to help her lift Eli. Eli's eyes rolled back in his head and he groaned.

"Eli! Speak to me!" Fiona begged.

Brian gave her an incredulous look. Myron whined piteously and started tearing down the door.

Eli clutched Fiona's hand. "Three things," he said weakly.

"What? What, darling?"

"One, I'll never leave you. Two, I want lots of children. And three..."

"Yes, Eli, what's the third thing?" Brian asked interestedly.

"I'll kill both of you if you ever pull a stunt like this again." And with that, he finally passed out.

Eleven

———

"The problem was that I'm not used to dealing with such total incompetence," Eli explained seriously to Brian as dawn painted the sky the following morning.

"Will you please stop pacing and sit down?" Fiona pleaded. Eli had a concussion, assorted bruises and a nasty cut on the back of his head in addition to his other injuries. The doctor had told him in no uncertain terms to go straight to bed and stay there for three days, but he wasn't obeying.

Brian and Fiona had called an ambulance and the sheriff after Eli had passed out. As soon as Eli regained consciousness, he had barely given the hospital staff time to patch him up before he rushed over to the sheriff's office to find out all he could about the prowler that had terrorized Oak Hill all through Christmas. Since Fiona had made Brian clean up the mess at the kennel while she went with Eli, the boy was now eager to hear all the details.

"Who is that guy?" Brian demanded. They were all in the lounge of the kennel, enjoying the first peace and quiet they had known for many hours.

"He's a private investigator hired by Mr. Snyder to find and, um, obtain Rocky," Fiona explained.

"He's a totally unscrupulous and incompetent private investigator whose license was revoked five years ago for unethical practices," Eli added with relish. "The lack of scruples and the remarkable level of incompetence were what made him so hard to nail."

"Why did Snyder hire him if he's operating without a license?" Brian wanted to know.

"He does cases cheap," Eli explained dryly.

"My guess is that the two men have a lot in common," Fiona added distastefully.

"What I don't get," Brian said, "is why he started breaking in here before Rocky ever arrived."

"That's the reason I never once suspected Rocky was the source of our troubles," Eli said with the air of a man vindicating himself. "Rocky arrived *after* this guy started hanging around."

"Well?" Brian prodded.

"Get this, Brian. This is unbelievable," Fiona interjected, since they were getting to her favorite part of the story. "Plain, ordinary-looking, middle-aged Mrs. Snyder ran off with a young male aerobics teacher—winner of the All-American Bulging Biceps Competition."

Brian gaped at her. "You can't be serious."

"I swear it on my life," Fiona assured him. "Anyhow, this was the beginning of a very nasty divorce between the Snyders. One day while Mr. Snyder and the kids were out, Mrs. Snyder snuck into the house and swiped Rocky on the grounds that he was rightfully her dog. Snyder started hassling her for the dog weeks ago. But after she and her boyfriend moved, Snyder couldn't find out where they were. So he hired this flatfoot." She kind of liked the way that word sounded.

"The incompetent flatfoot couldn't find out where they lived, either. But he *did* find out from the aerobics gym that they were going away to Hawaii together for Christmas," Eli continued. "Snyder knew that she'd have to leave the dog somewhere, and he told the flatfoot it would probably be here."

"So the rest of the story is one desperate, foiled attempt after another to bust Rocky out of here," Fiona said.

"Why did Snyder initially hire someone else to find out if the dog was here?" Brian asked.

"Would you believe that Mrs. Snyder managed to get a court order to keep her husband away from the dog?" Fiona said.

Brian whistled. "She must have pestered a lot of bureaucrats to get hold of something that ridiculous. To think that you take tax money out of my paycheck every week to finance that kind of thing!" He was clearly outraged.

"So Snyder's flatfoot came here the first night and found the side door open, thanks to Fiona," Eli said with a sharp glance at her. "He snuck into the kennel, waited for her to leave, and then started looking at her paperwork. Halfway home, Fiona realized she had left a door unlocked. She came back to lock it and double-check everything. The guy panicked, grabbed all her paperwork, and ran out the door with it."

"It gives me the creeps to think I was wandering around in the dark alone while he was here," Fiona admitted with a shiver.

"As soon as he realized Rocky's name wasn't among those files, he decided to return them. The next night he slipped in an open door just before the kids closed up, and left the papers where he had found them, hoping no one had noticed their absence." Eli shook his head. "It's the dumbest thing I ever heard of. Fiona might never have thought anything was wrong if he hadn't done that.

"Naturally, Snyder was having a fit over his lack of results, so the guy came back at midnight the following night.

But Fiona spotted him before he broke in, and he ran off again."

"So you see, I did have good reason to consult Morgan's," Fiona said smugly.

Eli's eyes glinted with rueful humor and something much stronger when he looked at her. Fiona's whole body came alive under that gaze.

"So, what then, guys?" Brian asked loudly.

"Hmm? Oh, so then I staked out the kennel. But, of course, that was the night you arrived and scared Fiona half to death. I ran out the door, leaving it wide open. He saw me, and he slipped in and tried to access the computer files.

"When that didn't work, the Snyders decided to come here themselves to ascertain whether or not the dog was here. If he was, their plan was to liberate him." Even now, Eli's face reddened at the humiliating memory. "That didn't work, but at least they could pinpoint exactly where Rocky was."

"Oh, no," Brian said. "Then we moved Rocky!"

"Exactly," Fiona said. "But if the detective had made his move immediately, he might have actually gotten Rocky."

"That's right," Brian said. "We had three quiet nights in a row. Why?"

Fiona glanced hesitantly at Eli before answering, "Because the detective was out of town, visiting his family for the holidays." Brian flashed a startled look at Eli, who felt even now that he'd like to murder the prowler for that one. Fiona cleared her throat and continued, "Anyhow, the detective returned to town late Christmas night and got straight back to work. He managed to break in here by crawling through the dog flap in Houdini's outside run. It left no trace of evidence. Eli *said* this place was as leaky as a sieve in terms of security. So, thinking he had Rocky, the man took Houdini with him."

Eli's eyes sparkled. "Can you imagine the conversation they must have had when Snyder told him it was the wrong dog?"

"That's why Snyder was so hysterical the second time he came here," Fiona said. "He thought we had lost, killed, or given away Rocky and that's why there was a different dog in his place."

"So they turned Houdini loose—"

"Just expecting him to survive on his own," Fiona interrupted furiously.

"That's when they started getting desperate. So the flatfoot came back again. This time he had a photo of Rocky and was prepared to search the whole damn kennel. He was about to break in when Fiona appeared. He followed hot on her heels." Eli shook his head in professional disgust.

"So when I retraced my steps, he hit me," she said.

"And panicked and ran when he heard Eli coming," Brian said.

"What I can't understand is the absolute stupidity that drove him to return last night," Fiona said with a frown. "You would think he would realize that we would take extra precautions after I was attacked."

"By last night I had finally figured out that we were dealing with someone of enormous stupidity and incompetence," Eli said smugly. "I still didn't know what he was after, but I was certain he'd fall for the oldest trick in the book—playing dead. And he did."

"Wow," Brian said solemnly. "Will he go to jail?"

"I sure hope so," Fiona said fervently. "He's been released on bail, but as soon as Vicky gets back, I'll show her Eli's report. Then she and her lawyer can work out the exact charges. Since Snyder has kids to take care of, I hope he just gets sentenced to community work. Hundreds of hours of it," she added. "Mrs. Snyder will probably make a few charges of her own. I gather the detective discovered which Hawaiian hotel she was staying at and they harassed her about Rocky by phone for days before she started refusing to accept any calls."

"Has the guy agreed to turn evidence against Snyder?" Brian asked. After Fiona nodded, he said, "I can't get over it. Our entire lives disrupted, even put into danger, because one dippy family is fighting for custody of one smelly, ugly, lazy dog with a thyroid condition."

"People can be irrational about pets," Fiona said simply.

"Everyone connected with Oak Hill is irrational," Eli said resignedly. "And may I remind you both that your lives wouldn't have been in danger last night if you had stayed put the way I told you to?"

"Hey, man, I tried to make her stay home. She wouldn't listen," Brian said defensively.

"I believe you." Eli turned a stern gaze upon Fiona.

"I couldn't just leave you to die alone in the dark!"

"Fi-ona. I am a professional. I had everything under control until you scared the life out of me by placing yourself right in front of that idiot's gun."

"E-lijah," she said crisply, "you were not in your normal tip-top condition last night, as we both know. And instead of standing here scolding me for trying to save your hide, you should be in bed."

"So should you, Fifi," Brian reminded her.

Eli considered it. "Well, if we're *both* in bed, I guess it won't be so boring."

"This is getting good," Brian said.

"Leave us alone, Brian." Eli nodded toward the door.

"I don't know," Brian said. "You've both got concussions. Are you sure I shouldn't—"

"Out," Fiona said, her eyes locked with Eli's.

Brian smirked. "Now don't do anything too strenuous, kids."

"Split," Eli said without taking his gaze from Fiona's face.

"I'd love to stay, but duty calls," Brian said. As a parting shot he added, "I guess we'll be seeing a lot of you from now on, Eli."

Eli continued to stare at Fiona after Brian's departure. His eyes had a glint of determination in them, mingled with the relentless awareness that had existed between them from the first.

Fiona twisted her hands nervously. "So the case is over." Her voice sounded breathless to her own ears.

"Yeah. Now we can talk about more important things," he informed her.

Her heart fluttered uncomfortably. Now was the time to tell him. Before he hopped into his car and drove off. *Now.* "I . . . I really haven't been at my best since we met, Eli."

"Really?" he murmured, stalking forward.

She backed away, wanting him to understand. "Yes. You see, Christmas always brings out the worst in me. I feel...you know, all alone. And I've been worried sick about the prowler, so I've been a little tense and self-absorbed."

"Uh-huh." He followed her slowly around the couch.

"And I've been so overworked that I'm awfully tired, and I know I must look terrible. Usually, my face wouldn't frighten small children," she joked feebly.

"I've always thought you were so beautiful a man would cut off his arm for the right to touch you," he said.

That stopped her. She swallowed. "Really?"

"Yes. And if this is what you're like at your worst, then I'm a lucky man."

"You are?" She tilted her head back as he drew near. "Do you . . ." She licked her lips. His warm gaze caught the movement and focused on her mouth. "Do you remember what you said last night?"

"Something about killing you and Brian."

"Yes. And . . ."

"Lots of children."

"Yes," she said encouragingly as his arms slid protectively around her. When he lowered his head to kiss her, she touched his cheek with her fingers and said, "I've got to hear the most important one."

"I'll never leave you," he promised with all his heart.

"Oh, Eli, I love you," she said at last. The longing of years was in the kiss she gave him, and the possessive love in his embrace filled her with certainty. Yes, he would stay. She believed him.

His breath fanned her face when he pulled away. He hugged her tightly, cherishing the strength hidden in her fragile body. "I haven't exactly been at my best, either," he admitted wryly. "Last night I finally had my chance to rescue you, and instead you had to cart me off to the hospital."

"You were a hero," she assured him earnestly. She pressed her body against him and stifled a laugh. He was very excited. "Maybe we'd better go home," she suggested.

"Good idea," he mumbled against her hair. As he helped her into her coat, he said, "We've got to move."

"What?"

"Counting Bundle, there will be seventeen of us, Fiona. We can't live in that little cottage, and I've only got an apartment. And by the way," he added sternly, "Bundle is the last one. No more, Fiona. I can't handle it."

"Of course, Eli," she said placidly, not meaning it for a moment. He was, after all, a man who took in strays. "Obviously you're not including the children we're going to adopt."

"Well, no, they're a little different from dogs." He studied her suspiciously. She had agreed too readily to his ultimatum. "I think adoption's a great idea, but I want to have a baby, too."

"*You* won't be having it," she reminded him. She walked out the front door and took his gloved hand in her mitten as they headed for the oak grove.

"No," he admitted. "But I'll be a great coach, don't you think?"

She laughed at his smug tone. "You'll be pushy and bossy and rude. And you're so squeamish you'll probably keel over."

"And *you're* supposed to be in love with me," he complained.

"I am," she assured him. "And as soon as we get home, you won't have any room for doubt."

His whole body throbbed at the look in her eyes. "Oh, Fiona." He sighed. He slid his arm around her and pulled her close as they continued walking slowly. "You almost make me forget that my body feels like it's been run through a cement mixer."

"I'll kiss every inch and make it better," she promised.

As they neared the cottage he asked her, "How soon will Vicky be home?"

"Next week. Why?"

"This is supposed to be my vacation," he reminded her, a teasing light in his eyes. "So maybe when she gets back, you can get a few days off and we'll go to Wisconsin together."

"Wisconsin?" She stopped in her tracks.

"Yeah. You're marrying into a big family, Fiona. You might as well start meeting some of them."

"Will they like me?" She bent her head over the lock on her front door to hide her nervousness from him. Naturally it didn't work. He turned her to face him as soon as they were inside.

"They'll love you," he assured her seriously. He grinned. "As maddening as you are, they'll love you anyhow."

She was filled with warmth to think of how different her life would be from now on. All because of him. "I'm so glad you're the kind of man that takes in strays," she murmured as he started unbuttoning her coat.

"You're not a stray, Fiona. If it's the last thing I do, I'll make you stop thinking about yourself that way. You're the woman I love, and I love you because you have more life and warmth and generosity pouring out of you than the sun."

She slipped past his hands to lean against him and rest her head against his chest, too moved to speak. A moment later his arms tightened around her, sheltering and comforting, supportive and encouraging.

"You made a home for yourself here," he whispered. "You made all these people love you and care about you. I want to share that with you, just like I want you to share the family I have. And we'll also share the family we're making together." He chuckled a moment later. "Fifteen pets and a few kids."

She gasped. "We have to go back for Bundle! I want you to bring him here right away so he knows he has a home now."

"Later," Eli said, removing her coat.

"But—"

"Later." He slipped his chilly hands under her sweater, her flannel shirt, and her long underwear. Her muscles contracted involuntarily, then started to relax as he warmed his hands against her skin.

"You're not doing your fair share," he chided. "What happened to all those promises you made on the way here?"

"Oh. Yes," she breathed. She pulled off her mittens and started unzipping, unfastening and unbuttoning with trembling fingers. When she found the hard, muscled heat of his body under layers of clothing, she made a tiny moan of longing and stood up on tiptoe to kiss him.

He murmured to her, telling her how much he loved her, how much he craved her touch, how good all the days and nights together would be for the rest of their lives.

By the time he lifted her in his arms and carried her into the bedroom, Fiona agreed that Bundle could wait a few more hours.

"So," he whispered against her bare stomach as they lay sprawled across her bed. "Still hate Christmas?"

"All things considered, it wasn't so bad this year." Her eyes gleamed with the memory of their private celebration. "I guess if I'm with you I could even learn to like it."

He kissed her abdomen and flicked his tongue across her navel. A few moments later he asked, "Do you like that?"

"Ohhh, yes," she sighed, feeling reality whirl away from the two of them. She curled up to take his battered but still gorgeous face between her palms. "Your stamina is amazing. You should be unconscious instead of—"

"I'll be unconscious later, I promise."

She smiled and slid against him while their hands freely explored each other's bodies. She knew she should feel weak and exhausted after running around all night with a concussion, but she had never felt so wonderful in her life.

"Just think," she whispered, "if it weren't for the Snyders, we might never have met."

Eli stilled. "You know, I never thought of it that way." He grinned. "I guess we'll have to send them a Christmas card every year."

Fiona thought that was going a little too far, but at the moment, she and Eli had far better things to do than argue about the Snyder family.

*   *   *   *   *

Silhouette Special Edition®

proudly presents
the long-awaited "prequel" volume of

★ LOVE AND GLORY ★

by
LINDSAY McKENNA

Dawn of Valor

In the summer of '89, Silhouette Special Edition premiered three novels celebrating America's men and women in uniform: LOVE AND GLORY, by bestselling author Lindsay McKenna. Featured were the proud Trayherns, a military family as bold and patriotic as the American flag—three siblings valiantly battling the threat of dishonor, determined to triumph . . . in love and glory.

Now, discover the roots of the Trayhern brand of courage, as parents Chase and Rachel relive their earliest heartstopping experiences of survival and indomitable love, in

Dawn of Valor, Silhouette Special Edition #649.

This February, experience the thrill of LOVE AND GLORY—from the very beginning!

DV-1

Silhouette Books®